A Candlelight Ecstasy Romance®

"ARABY, COME DOWN OFF THAT HIGH HORSE OF YOURS AND I'LL TEACH YOU MORE THAN SOUTHERN MANNERS."

"You're crude, Daul McNeal!" She wanted to resist him but the inexorable hurricane of sensuality that surrounded him swept her toward him. Her only defense was her sharp tongue. "You couldn't teach me anything, you country bumpkin!"

Daul grinned maddeningly. "I could teach you about good old-fashioned passion and the joys of desire."

"I'd have trouble learning anything from you. We have absolutely nothing in common, especially not passion!"

"How would you know? I don't think you've ever experienced it."

"You don't know what I've experienced," Araby retorted sharply.

"You haven't experienced this," he said as he drew her against him and captured her lips with his.

CANDLELIGHT ECSTASY ROMANCES®

LOVE IS ALL
THAT MATTERS

Tate McKenna

A CANDLELIGHT ECSTASY ROMANCE®

Published by
Dell Publishing Co., Inc.
1 Dag Hammarskjold Plaza
New York, New York 10017

Dell ® TM 681510, Dell Publishing Co., Inc.

Candlelight Ecstasy Romance®, 1,203,540, is a registered
trademark of Dell Publishing Co., Inc., New York, New
York.

ISBN: 0-440-15006-X

Printed in the United States of America

First printing—November 1985

*To Vicki, who has shared
the agonies and the ecstasies
of this crazy, wonderful business.*

To Our Readers:

We have been delighted with your enthusiastic response to Candlelight Ecstasy Romances®, and we thank you for the interest you have shown in this exciting series.

In the upcoming months we will continue to present the distinctive, sensuous love stories you have come to expect only from Ecstasy. We look forward to bringing you many more books from your favorite authors and also the very finest work from new authors of contemporary romantic fiction.

As always, we are striving to present the unique, absorbing love stories that you enjoy most—books that are more than ordinary romance. Your suggestions and comments are always welcome. Please write to us at the address below.

Sincerely,

The Editors
Candlelight Romances
1 Dag Hammarskjold Plaza
New York, New York 10017

CHAPTER ONE

Rejection!

The word crawled through Araby Gilbert's head, refusing to leave or to be forgotten. Even though it had happened last week the wound was still fresh. And Araby had made the fatal mistake of not sending her material back out immediately. The collection of poems was here to remind her they would not be in print when school convened in a few weeks.

With a heavy sigh she looped a hemp rope on her arm and carefully climbed the steep stairs to the attic. Today Araby tackled the most difficult of chores, that of sorting through her beloved Aunt Lucy's worldly goods. The close, musty smell of the attic accosted her nostrils and gave her the sensation that she was about to sneeze. But she didn't, and the feeling was quite heady and uncomfortable.

Her mind kept wandering back to her collection of poems, perhaps because she didn't want to think about clearing out Aunt Lucy's things, and she went about her project a little distractedly.

Just how important was it that she have her poetry published? The university expected its professors to publish and gain distinction in their fields. It was also a matter of pride to Araby. When she went back to school she would have to face B. Nettington Goodfield, self-appointed poet laureate of Vanderbilt University who had self-published his first collection of poems, then pursuaded some obscure university press to publish the next. Hell, she could have self-published hers, if she had the money.

But Araby Gilbert didn't have the money.

What she had was an inherited farm in the middle of Tennessee that she had to sell. And the contents, which had belonged to her dearly beloved Aunt Lucy, had to be sorted and packed, then sold or given away. Although Araby needed the money she knew she would probably just donate what she couldn't use or keep. It seemed a sacrilege to sell Aunt Lucy's possessions. Araby could almost hear her aunt saying, in that sassy voice of hers, *It's just old stuff! Don't be possessed by your possessions!*

Araby crouched beside the old leather and brass, humpbacked trunk, stuffed the end of the rope through the handle, and square-knotted it. The only thing she remembered from her Girl Scout days was the chant on how to make a square knot:

To square a knot
good and tight,

12

right over left,
left over right.

Araby tested the knot by pulling as hard as she could and grunted in satisfaction. There, that should hold the massive piece of luggage, which she'd referred to as "the treasure chest" when she was a child. On rainy days she would go through its contents asking Aunt Lucy a million questions and trying on some of the clothes. *Life is a treasury,* Aunt Lucy used to say. And that was the theme of one of Araby's poems, one that had been rejected.

Actually it wasn't a matter of life or death if her poetry wasn't published. But there was an unspoken "publish or perish" code around the university English department. B. Nettington Goodfield would say, "Unfortunately, my dear, rejection is a part of the creative process." God, she hated that part of it. And she hated him for telling her that every time her poems were rejected.

Rejection. What an ugly word, she thought. It sounded like a contagious disease. Don't touch rejection! You might catch rejectionitis! The first time her poems were returned she had received an impersonal note stating something about them not being "right for us." She had wondered if anyone had even read her work. This time, though, someone definitely had taken the time to read them and comment that one, in particular, was "too schmaltzy." That really hurt.

Araby looked around the attic for something heavy enough to act as a pulley. Perhaps that old cast-iron wood stove. She scooted across the floor to its dusty base and circled the black potbellied heater with the other end of her rope. She pulled, testing her strength and that of the stove. Maybe she should wait until her neighbor Mr. Gosset arrived. He and his son could help her with this project before they loaded the hay.

Curling her arm around her forehead, Araby blotted the grimy perspiration onto the sleeve of her clean blouse. Her exacting blue eyes darkened when she noted the smudges already there, and she primly flicked a ball of dust from her firmly pressed jeans. With the back of her hand she pushed a lock of blond hair away from her forehead, but stubbornly it fell back.

Damn! It wasn't quite ten in the morning, and she was a filthy mess! Lord, it was hot and humid in this attic! Mr. Gosset said they'd have rain by afternoon and promised to come over early. So where was he? Araby sat down on the dirty floor and leaned against the age-blackened stove, completely unaware that smudges now covered her shoulders. Her blended-silk button-down blouse would never be the same.

Her mind returned to her stunted literary career. There was even a book on the subject of rejection. It was in the library, right alongside books on how to write for publication, rearing its ugly back with the one-word title, *Rejection!* Of course it had caught her eye, and Araby had snapped it up. After all, it was her disease wasn't it?

14

The book was full of wonderful, supposedly encouraging facts about great writers who had been rejected. James Joyce, e. e. cummings, and Dr. Seuss had encountered many rejections. Then there was Emily Dickinson. How well Araby knew about dear Emily, who saw only seven of her poems published in her lifetime. And now people like Araby made their living studying her work. But why hadn't Emily persisted and sent her work to other periodicals, the way Walt Whitman had when he was rejected? The unanswerable question. Maybe that was why Emily had been a recluse. She couldn't face the world and its ugly rejections.

Well, Araby wouldn't accept those rejections! She would send her poems elsewhere. First thing tomorrow!

She cocked her head and listened for the sound of a truck on the seldom-used country road that ran in front of the farm house. *Where was Mr. Gosset?* Araby felt as though she were frying in the airless attic. She couldn't waste any more time on this project. She examined her rope system. There was no reason why she couldn't make this work by herself.

Bracing her back against a nearby iron bedstead, she shoved the trunk to the edge of the stairs with her feet. Grasping the rope, she let it slide carefully through her hands, then tipped the trunk over the stairs' sharp incline with her toe. For about twenty seconds she and the cast-iron-stove pulley held the weight of the loaded, humpbacked trunk suspended on the staircase. She let it descend slowly, even though the rope was beginning to burn her hands.

As is usually the case, the disaster happened fast. It started when the black potbellied stove stopped acting as pulley for the weighty trunk and began to slide then lunge rapidly toward the stairs. Of course Araby wasn't strong enough to hold the trunk by herself. But she tried.

Later she realized if she had just released the rope and let the trunk and stove fall, she wouldn't have been whipped against the stove and dragged down the path of least resistance. But Araby held on to the rope for dear life and followed the humpbacked trunk and cast-iron stove all the way to the bottom of the stairs. Fortunately she rolled behind the heavy items and didn't bang her head until she landed at the very bottom. It all happened so quickly, she didn't even have time to scream before everything went black.

He knelt beside her, his dark, devil eyes drinking in her pale beauty, his strong, sure hands roaming over her body. She looked different from the last time he had seen her, more vulnerable, softer. He liked that in a woman. Softness. And sensitivity combined with intelligence. She had all three, this lovely college professor with the lofty-sounding title of doctor. He pushed her blond hair back and caressed her forehead. Her eyelashes were sorrel fringes against high cheekbones, a sign of good breeding, he mused. Her nose was too short to be classic, her mouth too wide to be a precise cupid's bow. But she was damned attractive, even seductive, as she lay with her mouth slightly open.

She moved and moaned softly; her eyelashes fluttered. He hovered closer, looking down at the pale creature who lay at the bottom of the stairs.

Araby strained through glazed, aquamarine eyes trying to focus on the dark, masculine figure hovering over her. A cold, wet cloth flopped down on her forehead, and she closed her eyes again to avoid the dripping water. "Ooooh," she groaned. "Am I dead?"

"I don't think so," the male voice answered. "Apparently, no broken bones. Just a few bruises."

"Mr. Gosset?" Araby struggled to lift a limp hand to her head and remove the sloppy, wet thing that dribbled water down her face and around to the back of her neck. Her eyes focused slowly, then widened with alarm as the double image slowly turned into one rugged, male silhouette, obviously *not* the sixty-year-old Leon Gosset. "Who are you?" Araby asked, alarmed.

"Daul McNeal. You okay?"

"I'm fine. Just who the hell are you? Dow-well who?" she repeated, mimicking his Southern accent. "And what are you doing here in my house?" Araby attempted to rise up on bruised elbows but groaned aloud as pains shot through her shoulders and head.

The man, who could easily be mistaken for a

runaway hobo from the nearest rail yard, shoved her back down. "You'd better lie still and rest awhile. You were out cold for a minute or two."

"Get your hands off me! I'm perfectly fine! Now move and let me up." Araby's heart pounded hard against her breast, and she grasped the thick male wrist attached to the huge hand that rested on her shoulder. It didn't move and neither did she.

Oh Lordy! He's pinned me to the floor, and I'm physically incapable of defending myself against this sex maniac! It's going to happen to me—right here—in my own place! What can I use to defend myself? She bent her leg, thinking first of the old knee-in-the-groin trick. Maybe she could jab him, then run. . . .

"Oh no! I'm going to be sick!" Frantically Araby clasped the sloppy wet dishcloth to her mouth while the man reversed his action and pulled her roughly to her feet. He steered her to the nearest door, the front door, through which he had just entered, and to the edge of the porch, where she hung her head over the side and heaved.

"This often happens with a head injury," he explained patiently, waiting for her to finish.

Araby held on to the side of the house and took deep breaths, hoping she now looked sufficiently repulsive to put off this sex maniac. After all, who wanted to rape a nauseated woman? Why didn't she take those karate lessons when they were offered on campus last spring? She took a determined breath. Now that she was outside on the front porch, she definitely would not be maneuvered back into the house. She wiped her mouth daintily, then turned to face the stranger.

"And now you get off my property before I call the cops." Her aquamarine eyes looked as cold as steel beneath the thick sorrel lashes. She was damn mad and wanted him to know it.

In arrogant defiance of her display of temper, the stranger's gray eyes gazed lazily around the placid oak- and magnolia-treed yard, then beyond to the country road that ran in front of the remote farm, going nowhere in particular over the Tennessee countryside. Eventually it led to Nashville.

"Don't see any signs of cops around the corner. How do you propose to call one?" he mused sardonically. His mouth quirked into a grin, half hidden by the three-day growth of a dark beard along his chin and jawline. The jarring eyes softened as he smiled and his dark hair fell casually over his forehead and curled along his shirt collar. Strands of gray in his hair indicated his age to be mid- to late thirties. Even if he hadn't pinned her to the floor, his unkempt appearance was enough to make anyone leery.

"Get out of here!" she grated, fully aware that he was right. She'd have to place a call and wait until the county sheriff could be located and persuaded to show up way out here. Lord, *anything* could happen! Repeatedly!

He folded his hands and stood with legs apart, gazing blatantly at her. "Is this the thanks I get for trying to save your life?"

"Saving my life?" she sneered. "I know what you were trying to do!"

He ignored her insinuation. "I just walked up to the door and heard this gawd-awful noise. Next thing I knew, things were flying down the stairs with you right after them. Sorry I didn't get there in time to prevent you from hitting your head. Don't you think you'd better lie down awhile?"

"Oh no, you don't! I'm just fine, standing right here!" Araby edged closer to the porch railing. If necessary she could bolt over the side and run. . . .

He smiled. "Okay. Anything you say, Fancy Lady," he drawled and allowed his eyes the freedom to calculate her assets, from the loose blond hair to the smudged blouse that clothed her firm, high breasts to her trim waist to the once neatly pressed jeans that embraced her rounded hips.

Before Araby could tell him what an impudent jerk he was for leering at her that way, the phone rang. Instead she said, "If you know what's good for you, you'll leave while I answer that. I intend to tell whoever is on that phone that a stranger is here."

"Tell them I'm one of your students, here for private poetry lessons." There was a touch of amusement in his voice that infuriated her. In addition to which, he obviously knew far too much about her.

She eyed him closely, taking in the steel-gray eyes, the aquiline nose, the scraggly beard. "You aren't one of my students."

20

"Sure I am. We met in your poetry workshop this summer. We made a deal. You said I could rent your country place in September, only I couldn't reach you in Nashville by phone. You'd better answer that. It's still ringing."

Araby hesitated. Maybe he *was* the one she offered to rent the place to. But he certainly hadn't looked like this at her poetry workshop! "You stay here. I'll be right back." Eyeing him warily, she stepped into the hall and lifted the old-fashioned black dial phone that rested on a yellowed hand-crocheted doily.

Ignoring her threats, Daul McNeal slipped casually inside the screen door and walked over to the bottom of the stairs. He set the wood stove upright and pushed it into a corner so it would be out of the way, and did the same with the trunk. When Araby returned from her phone conversation she was appalled that this man would defy her request to stay outside.

"I thought I said—"

"Look, I don't know what your problem is, Fancy Lady, but I'm not here to harm you. I'm here to rent a room. It's nearly September, and we made an agreement."

"Well, you can't stay right now because I'm here. I have at least another week's worth of work to do yet. You can rent it when I leave."

"Nope. No good. I need it now."

"I'm sorry, you can't have it. I'm staying here and have no intention of renting it to you now." She propped her hands on her hips to emphasize

21

her words, and his eyes dropped to admire her smooth curves. Somehow his glance took the punch out of her assertiveness, and it further irritated her.

"Did I hear you say you need help getting that hay stored in the barn today?"

"You listened in on my phone conversation!" she accused.

He shrugged. "You were just in the next room. How could I miss?"

Reluctantly, she reconsidered. Araby thought of the hay, baled and lying in the fields. It was already sold, and damn, she needed the money. It would help pay the mounting inheritance taxes on this place. If the bales got wet they would be ruined and worthless. Admittedly, she needed help now. For some reason she unburdened her present problem to the stranger, who was becoming more appealing by the minute.

"Mr. Gosset, a neighboring farmer, had promised to bring his son over and collect the baled hay for me. He just called to say he hurt his back and his son has gone to Crossville to see about a job. I'll have to wait until tomorrow for them to stack the hay. But tomorrow may be too late."

"It'll probably rain today," Daul commented quietly. "If those bales get wet, they won't be worth much."

"That's just what I was thinking. Uh, could you do it? I'll pay you well," she proposed.

"I'd be glad to help you out," Daul replied. "Just rent me a room in exchange for a day's work. Or

I'll pay for the room if you want. I don't need much space, only a bed, and won't bother a soul."

Araby studied the man silently, considering his counterproposal.

"You see," he went on to explain, "I'm under contract to write a batch of songs for a movie. That's all I want to do." He shrugged his hands, palms out, and Araby's eyes dropped to take in his long fingers. The action was a motion of contrition. He was appealing to her softer side.

She pushed that same aggravating lock of blond hair back again and sighed heavily, feeling the country squeeze he was applying. She had met others like him. Smart and wiley, while appearing to be a country bumpkin. "You said you were a song writer. What . . . what is your name? I didn't catch it. And what have you written?" Araby wondered why she bothered to ask what he'd written. She wouldn't recognize it anyway.

"Daul McNeal. Do you need references? I can supply plenty from Nashville, people in the business who have worked with me for years. Some of my biggest hits have been 'You're My Desire,' 'Don't Leave Town Without Me,' and 'A Simple Love Song.'"

Araby didn't want to admit that she'd never heard any of his songs, so she countered him again. "Then why don't you stay in Nashville to write? Why do you have to go off hunting some country farm to stay in?"

He shrugged. "Too many friends in Nashville. They don't let me alone. And, this time, I have to be alone. Got to write under pressure. Anyway, it feels good to get back out here in the country. You can take the boy out of the country, but can't take the country out of the boy."

"What about the man?" She folded her arms. The man in him had scared the hell out of her a few minutes ago. What made her think that threat was over?

"The man needs a room in the country. And I'll pay you five hundred for the month."

Araby caught her breath. "F-five hundred for a room? Here?" She glanced around the room filled with antiques of dubious worth and *objets de junque* from another era.

"I need it badly. Anyway, I assume I'll have the whole place to myself when you leave. It's worth it to me to have uninterrupted privacy."

She shook her head. "I may regret this, but I'll give you a chance. There's a spare room in the attic where you can stay. It's a little dusty up there, but I suppose it'll do."

His face split into a victory smile. "Great! Now let's get to that hay before it rains."

She showed Daul the tractor parked in the end of the huge barn. The flatbed was already attached, ready for Mr. Gosset and son.

"Do you feel up to driving the tractor?" he asked as he checked the connection of the two large farm implements.

"Me? Why . . . I hadn't planned on it."

Daul raised his eyebrows. "Well, I certainly can't drive the tractor and load hay at the same time. It would take me about two weeks to do the job." He gestured to the billowing white clouds rising against a deep blue sky. "I figure we've got less than four hours until this thing breaks."

Her eyes followed his to the threatening sky. "It's been a long time since I've driven a tractor, but I suppose I could do it."

"It'll all come back to you, just like riding a bike. Are you sure you feel up to it?"

Araby brushed off his concern. "I'm fine. Let's get this job done before it rains."

So Araby Gilbert, Ph.D. in English with a specialty in the work of Emily Dickinson, rolled up her silk-blended sleeves and climbed onto the hard metal seat of the old tractor. Daul McNeal, songwriter of country-music distinction, peeled off his shirt, hopped aboard the flatbed, and gave Araby the high sign. They spent the remainder of the day loading and hauling hay bales from the fields to the barn. They didn't even take time to eat lunch.

As the final bales were being tossed high in the barn's corner, raindrops could be heard falling on the old tin roof.

"Thank goodness, it's all in!" Araby exclaimed happily. "We beat the rain! I don't know what I would have done without your help, Daul."

"Without you to drive the tractor, I couldn't have done it, either, Araby. It isn't a one-person job. We make a good team."

"Well, I appreciate your hard work, Daul. Thank you," she said generously.

25

He motioned to the corner of the barn. "Did you know you have a freeloader in here?"

"What?" She squinted into the dark corner he indicated but could see nothing.

"A little calico behind the corn bin. Acts scared. See his eyes gleaming?"

"A stray cat!" Araby muttered scornfully. "What's that thing doing in here?"

"Must be a little runaway, seeking refuge."

Araby refused to show concern for the scraggly animal. "Well, I'm cold and would rather seek refuge in the house!" With a shriek she dashed across the yard through the chilling Tennessee rain. Daul followed and, like her, left his shoes on the screened-in back porch.

Araby fixed them a glass of iced tea, then disappeared to take a warming shower, forgetting about her boarder.

Daul poured himself another glass of iced tea, wishing it was a cold beer. She obviously didn't expect to have a man around the house. At least not a beer-drinking man. He wandered through the small farmhouse listening to the rhythm of the raindrops falling on the tin roof, then decided to bring in his luggage. When Araby eventually entered the living room, fresh and clean, Daul was picking out a few chords on Aunt Lucy's old upright piano.

"You're the first one who's played that piano in years," she murmured softly. "It's just an old wreck."

"No, it isn't." Daul's hand caressed the engraved

26

walnut console. "It's just badly out of tune. Otherwise, the instrument is in fine shape."

He rose, still clad in his drenched jeans and no shirt. Araby tried to keep her eyes on his and not think of his fine masculine shape. "Well, I don't know much about pianos. It just sounds so awful, I figured it wasn't worth tuning. Would you, ah, like to take a shower?"

"You bet," he said with a grin. "It would be more pleasant for everyone around me."

Her eyes inadvertently traveled up his torso, trying not to linger over the smattering of dark hair across the muscular definition of his chest. "Meaning me, since I'm the only one around?"

"You got it."

She handed him a couple of towels. "There's a small bathroom with shower down the hall and to the left."

He took the towels she offered, then paused. "Can I ask you something?"

Araby raised her eyebrows.

"What were you doing with that heavy stove and that huge trunk on the stairs? Just curious, you understand." He tried to hide a creeping grin.

She smiled contritely. "I was trying to haul the trunk downstairs so I could go through its contents out of the dust and heat of the attic." She paused, realizing that that was exactly where she planned to stick her songwriting boarder. "I used the cast-iron stove as a pulley. Unfortunately, the stove wasn't quite heavy enough to hold, and when it gave away, so did I."

27

"Why didn't you—"

"Turn loose of the rope?" Araby finished with a wry smile. "It just happened so fast, I didn't have time to think of that. Until later."

"Well, you accomplished your goal," he conceded. "The trunk's down here. How are you feeling now?"

"Okay. A slight headache. I suppose I should thank you for being here and trying to help."

"You're lucky. It could have been more serious if that stove had fallen on you."

Araby's eyes dropped and caught the small duffel bag and a battered guitar case by the door.

"Tools of the trade," he commented lightly. "Hope you don't mind a little guitar music."

Araby eyed the instrument warily and wondered what she was getting herself into. It suddenly occurred to her that there was now a man living in the house, a boarder, and there were things she should do. "I suppose I should show you to your room. And get it cleaned up a bit."

He reached for his baggage. "Don't bother. I'll do that. Up these stairs?"

She nodded. "You won't mind if I don't climb those stairs again today?"

"Don't blame you a bit. Uh, sheets? Are they already up here?"

"No. The mattress is covered with a canvas drape to keep out the dust, but I'll have to get your sheets." Araby stepped to the hall closet and returned with a set of linens, somewhat yellowed with age, but with elaborately decorated edges. "I hope you don't mind sleeping on crocheted sheets. My aunt decorated them. They're all that's here to use."

Her hand caressed the tiny stitches that constituted the pale yellow ruffles along the top edge of the sheet and pillow-case ends. Oh Lord, the hours of work it took. She could still remember Aunt Lucy's knobby fingers flicking the silver crochet needle around the thread, making her beautiful crocheted edging. She was always busy with something.

His voice was low. "I don't mind. Do you?"

"Huh?" Araby's blue eyes lifted to touch his gray ones.

"Mind if I use these gilded sheets. Don't you have some old ones for me?"

"No. This is all. I mean, everything has her crocheting on it."

"Okay. Thanks. I'll take care of making my own bed."

Araby nodded silently, for she had no intention of making his bed. She tucked the sheets under his elbow and watched him take the stairs to the attic two at a time. Crazily, her mind roved to the mental image of this man sprawled across Aunt Lucy's sheets, the crocheted edges intimately flicking his bare skin.

She turned away from the stairs quickly and caught sight of the trunk of treasures she had planned to unload today. Well, it would have to wait until tomorrow. Right now she should fix a little supper. After all, she had a man in the house. And he had just done a day's work for her.

Araby puttered happily in the kitchen, humming the overture from *Romeo and Juliet* by Tchaikovsky while Daul showered. With considerable pride she fixed salads for each of them and warmed up the leftover quiche, cutting it into decorative triangles. When she heard the shower stop she poured the iced tea. By the time she had the small meal prepared, Daul stood in the doorway, fresh and clean-smelling, with damp, dark hair curling around his ears.

She looked up expectantly, but before a smile could form, her chin fell to her chest. Emblazoned across his tattered but clean sweatshirt were the faded words "Music City, U.S.A. Where Songwriters Do It with One Hand on the Piano."

"Like it?" he asked proudly with a rakish grin.

"It's . . . why it's absolutely crude!" she sputtered, her cheeks flushing with embarrassment.

"It is?" He looked down at the shirt as if he had never read the words before in his life. "Well, Fancy Lady, sorry if you're offended. But this is one of my most favorite shirts. Really gets me in the mood, if you know what I mean. It's one of only two I brought along, so you'll be seeing it a lot."

"My name is Araby Gilbert, not *fancy lady,*" she sniffed. "I see you came prepared to be a gracious guest."

"Look here. I didn't come prepared to be any kind of guest. I came up here to write songs. And now that I've finished stacking the hay for you, that is exactly what I intend to do. After I eat."

"And I didn't expect you to come early and invade my privacy when I'm doing something so sentimental as packing away my dear, departed aunt's belongings."

"Am I infringing on your privacy or your emotional state, Doc-tor Gilbert? That's what your students call you, isn't it? Is it also what your friends call you? Your close, intimate friends? *Doctor.*"

Her eyes narrowed. "If we're going to make it together this week, and I'll remind you, you're in *my* house, you'd better cut the sarcasm, buster."

He took a step toward her. "The name's Daul, not buster. And, I'll remind you, *Doctor*, I just spent the better part of my day hauling hay for you and saving your financial ass on the deal."

Her contrite eyes shifted, then met his. He *had* helped her out today, and worked damned hard at it too. "My name's Araby, Daul. Not doctor."

He grinned, slow and devastating. His teeth gleamed white against the three-day growth of dark beard, and even in his rugged appearance there was very strong masculine appeal. "Okay, Araby. Now you're talking my language."

She took a shaky breath, wondering if the entire week would be like this. "Now that that's settled, would you like to eat a bite of supper with me . . . Daul?"

His eyes eagerly traveled over her shoulder. "Sure. I've worked up quite an appetite. And, with no lunch, I could eat a bear! What's this? Looks interesting."

"Quiche."

He sat down and, politely, refrained, with considerable effort, from commenting on the delicate meal.

Araby ate her quiche triangle and picked at her salad. She really wasn't very hungry tonight. Maybe the tumble down the stairs killed her appetite, or the fact that she'd never felt so tired after driving the tractor all afternoon. But Daul had hauled hay. He must be exhausted. She let her eyes roam over his squared shoulders, admiring the muscular body beneath the offensive sweatshirt.

Daul polished off the salad and ate his quiche triangle in record time. "That was delicious! You're a very good cook, Araby. Is there any more?"

She shook her head. "Sorry. That was the last of the leftovers."

"Mind if I check out the fridge and see if there's anything else to eat?"

"No. Help yourself." She watched as he searched the refrigerator, then the cupboards, in vain.

"What do you eat around here?"

"Oh, I don't know." She shrugged, trying to think what she'd had to eat all week.

"I guess so. Anyone with a waist as tiny as yours couldn't eat more than a few rose petals and a boiled egg."

"What! . . ." she gasped. He was making fun of her quiche, the ungrateful brute.

"Look, do you mind if I run down to the store and stock up on the kind of food I like?"

"No, but I hope you don't expect me to—"

He placed his palms on the table and braced his upper body as he leaned toward her. "I don't expect you to do a thing, Fancy Lady. I'm used to cooking. I'll do it myself. Want to go to the store with me? It might be the high point of your day!"

"No, thank you. I . . . I have a headache."

"Figures," he mumbled and lumbered out of the room. "And I'm still hungry from wrestling with those hay bales all day!"

"From the fall," she called after him. "I hit my head when I fell down the stairs today! That's why I have a headache!"

Her explanation fell on deaf ears as she heard him start the motor of his car and roar out of her driveway. Why was she bothering to explain to this bumpkin anyway? He was just a no-name country-music songwriter while she was the South's foremost authority on Emily Dickinson's poetry. There was no way the two of them could ever touch a common chord. *No way!*

CHAPTER TWO

Araby woke to sounds and smells that took her back to her childhood in this very house. The clinking of dishes. The oven door squeaking closed. The smell of bread baking and meat frying. Frying? She bounced up, remembering she had a house guest. Actually, a boarder. A man in the house! She grabbed a robe and swept into the kitchen.

"Do you know what time it is? What are you doing in the kitchen at this hour?" she demanded of the man who stood with his back to her. His shoulders seemed awfully broad and hips extremely narrow. Very masculine. It was nice to have a man around the house, fixing the morning coffee, preparing breakfast.

Daul turned around, long-handled fork in one hand, pot holder in the other. He was, for all the world, a picture of masculine domesticity. "And a jolly good morning to you too," he grated with a forced smile. "You certainly aren't very chipper in the morning, are you? Maybe a cup of coffee

34

would help. To answer your questions, it's 6:30 A.M., and I'm fixing breakfast. Care to join me?"

Araby tried to push her blond hair back, but it fell casually over one eye. She wore some kind of white lacy thing with long sleeves and looked very ethereal. Celestial, fragile, an angel in disguise, Daul mused. And damned appealing, even at this hour. At that moment he wanted to touch her, to see if she was as soft and gentle as she looked, to see if she was real.

The mood was broken as Araby spoke. "I don't usually eat breakfast. And certainly not at this hour of the morning."

He decided it must be her energy aura that was so strong. "Neither do I, but I'm awake and it seemed like a good idea at the time. Do you like biscuits and ham and red-eye gravy? With a side dish of grits?"

She cocked her head and her voice softened just a little. "It's been a long time since I've eaten a country breakfast like that. The coffee smells marvelous." She moved toward the perking pot. "Do you mind if I go ahead and have some?"

"Please, help yourself. It's your kitchen." He turned back to his chores at the stove.

"But your coffee." She knew he had bought coffee because she hadn't bothered with anything but instant since she'd been here. She sipped the strong brew. "Ah, very good. Well, since I'm awake, too, I may as well make the most of it. I have a lot of packing and sorting to do today."

She disappeared into her bedroom, which was

next to the kitchen, and Daul called, "I'll have breakfast ready by the time you get dressed."

Although she hadn't intended to eat breakfast, the aromas drifting from the kitchen into her bedroom created an appetite Araby seldom had in the morning. She slipped into her last clean, pressed pair of jeans and tugged a deep turquoise sweater over her head. Fluffing up her hair, she stopped just long enough to put a touch of mascara on the tips of her lashes. When she reentered the kitchen Daul was setting the table.

"Hope you're hungry." He placed a spoonful of grits on each plate and set a platter of fried ham slices between them. A tray of a dozen or so biscuits steamed away, sending their distinctive flavor wisping into the air. "And here's the ham gravy."

"Grits?" she observed with delight, then inadvertently repeated his comment of last night. "I'm positively starved. I could eat a bear!"

"Quiche triangles don't stay with you long. Try a slice of country ham," he offered with a wry smile.

She sat across from him at the old-fashioned, round pedestal kitchen table. Maybe this essence of country honesty that Daul exuded was what had made her agree to rent the place to him that day at the poetry workshop. That and her urgent need for money. Even beneath his raggedy appearance yesterday that same honest quality had shown through. Strangely, she trusted him. Today, for some reason, he didn't look quite so slovenly. The beard was beginning to fill out, and he looked ap-

36

pealingly rugged. She didn't even mind his "Song-writers Do It with One Hand on the Piano" sweat-shirt this morning.

"You know, Daul, I haven't had grits and red-eye gravy since I was a kid and Aunt Lucy used to fix them. And certainly not biscuits." Her South-ern breeding came to the fore as she made a little hole in the center of the grits and filled it with the deep-red ham gravy.

Daul opened up a biscuit and inhaled the savory aroma that rose from its middle. "Ahhh, there's nothing like that smell! I haven't had all this in a long time, either. But every once in a while I get the urge for some good ole down-home cooking. It's nice, though, to have someone around who appreciates it. Someone who actually likes grits! Do you know the secret to really good red-eye gravy?"

She shook her head. "I've never made it."

"Strong coffee. You use the strongest coffee you can get and stir it in the ham drippings until it's just right."

"Coffee, huh? Well, it's great. And your grits are prepared just right, not too sloppy." She took a bite of grits and broke open a biscuit. "Hmmm, light and fluffy. Made from scratch?"

"You bet! Takes a very light touch." He flexed the long fingers of one hand, and Araby thought of those hands and wondered if they had a light touch with everything.

"Where did you learn to cook like this, Daul?"

"Back on my grandpa's farm in Arkansas. I spent

every summer there, and Grandma taught me about country cooking. But Albert—he didn't want to be called anything but his name—prepared me for the really important things in life. Like how to toss hay. That came in handy just yesterday. And how to milk a goat. You never know when you'll run into a goat that needs milking." There was a lightness to his voice that Araby loved.

"Rest assured, there are no goats around here," she laughed.

"I wouldn't be too surprised, Fancy Lady." He ripped open another biscuit, put a slice of ham inside it, and bit into it, obviously savoring the mixture of flavors.

"Did your grandfather also teach you to play the guitar?"

Daul nodded. "Yep. We'd sit on the front porch evenings, and he'd play the harmonica while I learned my chords. . . ." He paused, remembering, then continued rapidly. "That's where I first heard 'The Grand Ole Opry' on WSM radio, every Saturday night. Albert refused to buy that new-fangled machine called the television, so we listened to Hank Williams and Ernest Tubb and Patsy Cline on the radio. Broke our hearts when she was killed in that plane crash."

"And I'll bet you wanted to be on 'The Grand Ole Opry' show when you grew up," Araby finished. "That story sounds familiar."

"No. As I grew older my desire to create music, not just sing it, took precedence. That and the fact that I can't sing very well. But I hear it in my head. So that's what goes down on paper."

"And so you made it big in Nashville."

"Well, it wasn't quite that easy, but, yes. I've been able to make a living from my songs. And what about you, Fancy Lady? What are you doing out here in the country? I hope you don't mind my saying so, but you look a little out of place."

She took a final bite of biscuit. "Oh no. I'm not really out of place. I grew up in the city, in Baltimore, but I, too, spent summer vacations here on the farm with my Aunt Lucy. She was my mother's oldest sister, and after my mother died, invited me down here every year. We had a wonderful time, and as I grew up she was the mother figure I needed. When she died a couple of years ago I just couldn't bring myself to come out here and pack away her stuff. Until now."

"What changed your mind?"

"Time. And taxes. As much as I'd like to keep it, I can't afford it. I'll clean out most of her things now and decide what to keep and what to give away. Then, next spring, when the market is better, I'll put the farm up for sale."

"Seems a shame to sell it."

"Yes. I know. But I just can't keep it. I work in Nashville and don't get out here that often. Also, it takes too much money to keep up a farm."

He nodded slowly. "I understand that too."

"Since you cooked breakfast, I'll clean up," Araby offered, scooting her chair back and taking a couple of plates to the sink.

39

Daul brought his plate and cup over. "I can help. It's my mess."

"No, I insist. You get to work. I'd like to pack away some of the kitchen items, anyway."

"Well, okay." Reluctantly, he started out of the kitchen.

"Daul?" She faced him with a faint smile. "Thanks for the breakfast. It brought back some very nice memories. And it was delicious."

His gray eyes sought hers for a split second. "Yeah. For me too." And he was gone, up the stairs two at a time. Within minutes she could hear random chords on a guitar. When she finished cleaning the kitchen and packing away a box of baking pans, she headed for the living room, unconsciously humming the tune Daul had begun to play repeatedly on the guitar.

"What are you doing?"

Araby looked up with a start and straightened, her face flushed from being bent over the trunk. "Trying to finish unloading the contents of this trunk. It's mostly old clothes. There are even some here that belonged to my Uncle John. And he's been dead over twenty years. I'm just going to give them away. . . . What's wrong? Hit a blank wall with your writing?"

"Aw, just not quite in the mood," Daul grumbled as he ambled around the room watching her fold the clothes into a paper bag. "Sometimes it takes a few days to get in the groove for writing. I tried to get a head start on the process by letting my hair go and growing this beard. But it hasn't worked yet."

"Letting your hair grow?" Araby laughed. "Are you a temperamental writer?"

"Aren't we all?"

Araby looked at him for a moment. Was he including her in that easily spoken "we"? "Do you mean you have to let your hair get shaggy and grow a beard before you can write?"

His hand scraped over the dark, bearded stubble thoughtfully. "It's a mental game I play with myself. Sometimes it helps to *feel* bohemian. Don't you think?"

"Me? Oh, I don't know." Araby didn't think she'd ever felt bohemian.

"What do you do to get yourself in the mood to write, Araby? Don't you feel better in a pair of old, broken-in jeans and an old sweatshirt?"

"One that says 'Songwriters Do It with One Hand on the Piano'?" she laughed.

"Or 'Poets Get It On in Iambic Pentameter,'" he teased, his gray eyes crinkling at the edges.

She shook her head and laughed with him. "What makes you think I write?"

"Doesn't everybody who studies English, and poetry in particular?"

"I guess so." She ducked her head. "But writing it and publishing it are two different things. I've done the former, but haven't been able to do the latter."

"Have you tried?"

"Oh, yes." She gave a halfhearted laugh. "Sev-

41

eral times. They keep coming back with interesting little notes attached."

"Where did you send them?"

"Mostly literary magazines. University presses, you know. Although I did send a batch to *Reader's Digest* one time, at Gerry's suggestion. But, they all came back home to roost."

"Gerry?"

"He's my . . . er, friend. Back in Nashville."

Daul's eyebrows raised and he read more into the word "friend" than she intended. *"Reader's Digest,* huh?"

She nodded and shrugged as if it didn't matter. But, of course, it did. And he knew it.

"So, what does Gerry know?"

"Not much about writers," she chuckled. "He's a comptroller at Vandy and thinks in very definite terms. Maybe my problem is that I haven't gotten myself in the right mood to write. Haven't gotten bohemian enough."

"Believe me, it helps."

"But you aren't like this all the time, Daul. You didn't look like this the day of the poetry workshop. You certainly didn't look like a shaggy dog that day." As she racked her brain Araby couldn't remember what he looked like that day. But she would never forget the way he looked now.

"It's probably all in my head, this getting in the mood to write." Daul started to stir around the room as he talked, occasionally stopping to absently check a faded picture on the wall or an ornamental knickknack. "This is the first time I've signed a contract to write more than one song, and the first time I've done a movie. Guess I feel the pressure."

"What's the movie about?" Araby examined each item she pulled from the trunk, then folded it away. She could tell Daul needed company. Maybe he just needed to talk his way out of this slump he seemed to be in.

"Briefly, it's about a successful country singer living in L.A. who goes back to his West Texas home for his parents' wedding anniversary party. It's a big deal, sort of a family reunion. He becomes reacquainted with his old girlfriend and realizes he's still in love with her. Trouble is, she's engaged to another man."

"What happens next?" Araby's hands rested in her lap as she sat on the floor, caught up in listening to Daul, forgetting about the clothes in the trunk.

"Well, they pick up where they left off in their romance. There'll be, you know, some love scenes. Then he, uh, goes back to Hollywood, but isn't happy there. He gets rid of his live-in girlfriend, insults his friends, and finally heads back to West Texas."

"And the girl?"

Daul grimaced and sat down on the sofa opposite her, dropping his hands between his widespread knees. "She gives the ring back to her fiancé and greets our hero with open arms. Sounds a little . . ."

"Schmaltzy?" Araby supplied the word readily. It was a word that stuck in her mind.

"Yeah. Schmaltzy, when you outline it like that. Course, by the time Hollywood and Clint Eastwood get through with it, I'm sure it'll be a smash."

"Along with, of course, your songs."

"Oh, yeah." Uneasily, Daul began to pace again.

Araby's hand dug into the trunk again and struck something hard buried deep amid the folds of clothing. Her fingers closed around the smooth object and she pulled it out of the trunk. "Oh, Daul, look! How beautiful!"

She held up a small wooden box carved in the shape of a heart. The light reflected a deep burgundy red from a circular knot formed by the wood grain in the center.

"Looks like cherry wood," he observed.

Araby rubbed her hand lovingly over the polished surface. "I've never seen this before. Wonder why . . ." She opened the palm-sized lid and smiled as the music box whirred and began to play "Let Me Call You Sweetheart." "How romantic. I wonder why Aunt Lucy never set this out among her other stuff. I'm sure she considered it among her most prized treasures."

"Maybe she wanted to protect it." Daul squatted nearby, letting his large, expressive hands dangle between his knees. "That doesn't really make sense, though, does it? Unless she wanted to keep it hidden."

Araby set the cherry-wood heart aside. "Maybe

44

she forgot about it." But it didn't look like the kind of thing one would forget.

Daul studied Araby's bent, blond head for a moment longer before he stood and walked over to the piano. Absently he plunked an off-key version of the music box's tune while Araby dug into the trunk again. A somber, silent mood had settled over them and they weren't sure why, but each receded into personal recollections.

Araby broke the mesmeric spell as she pulled another yellowed garment from the trunk. "It's Aunt Lucy's wedding dress. I have an old photograph of her in this very dress on her wedding day." She stood and pressed the Victorian-styled, lace and satin garment to her breast.

Daul looked at her askance for a long moment, his gray eyes hazy and distant. Suddenly his voice was commanding. "Try it on."

"What?" She lifted her eyes, startled by his request.

"Please. Try it on for me, Araby."

"W-why?"

He gazed at her and tugged thoughtfully at his bottom lip. "There's a scene in the movie where Eastwood stops by his aunt's house and she's fitting the wedding dress on his former girlfriend. When he sees her in this dress he knows he's lost her to another man. That seemed like a good place for a nice sad, lost-my-lover-type song to me. But I can't seem to get the feel for it. Maybe it's because I haven't seen many women in wedding dresses. So, would you?"

For some reason Araby nodded. "It might not fit me, you know. It belonged to my aunt over sixty years ago. She was a tiny little thing then."

He shrugged. "Doesn't matter. I just need to get an idea of the *feeling* a man would have seeing his lover in this dress."

Araby's smile grew slowly as she warmed to the prospect. "Okay, Mr. Songwriter. We'll do a little improv on the scene. When I return to this room I'll be the girlfriend who's going to marry another guy. And you're the man who—"

"—who realizes he's in love with her."

Her eyes flickered. There was something different in his voice, or was it just her imagination? "I'll be rat back," she said, affecting her best Southern accent. She swept away with the antique wedding dress.

Daul could hear the dress rustling. He imagined the yellowed lace slipping over Araby's head, nestling against her breasts, fitting her body tightly, swishing around her long legs. He grew a little hot thinking about her and walked around the room to try to take his mind off the way she would look.

Araby sailed through the door, an apparition from another era in the off-white, flowing dress, her blond hair pinned up to expose her slender neck and creamy white shoulders. Her aquamarine eyes were large and suddenly innocent. Daul's gaze froze on her. God, she was beautiful. The long sleeves, the tight bodice, the lace next to her breasts . . .

She moved into the room and revolved before

46

him with a swirl of her long skirt. "Purity," she said.

"Huh?"

"Purity. The white wedding dress used to stand for purity . . . that the bride was a virgin. I don't think it means that anymore."

He pursed his lips and stared. "No. I guess not."

Her hand reached to her heart. "I couldn't button it all the way." His eyes traveled to her hand and, sure enough, she had left the front of the dress open to reveal three inches of cleavage. "It's too tight in the bosom."

He took a step toward her, entranced. "It looks fine. Beautiful, in fact."

Araby stood perfectly still, caught by the obvious desire in his gaze. Her heart pounded beneath the tight bodice, and she could barely breathe. There was a tangible electricity in the air, a magnetic force growing in intensity between them. It was exciting, a feeling for a man that Araby had never before experienced. She wanted to reach out to him, to entice him to touch her.

"Do you think he would kiss her?" His voice was low and he stood close to her.

"W-what?"

"Clint Eastwood," Daul muttered. "In the movie. Do you think he would kiss his former girlfriend as she stood there in her wedding gown?"

"I don't know." Her eyes watched his, and they seemed to darken with a savage kind of passion. "Depends on how intimate they were in the past."

"Very." He moved closer. "You think he would

kiss her, even if she belonged to someone else now? Do you have another man, Araby?"

"There is," she choked, "someone I date."

"Gerry?"

She nodded silently.

"Is he a lover?"

"Yes—no," she answered breathlessly. Well, was Daul going to stand there all day, looking and not touching? She *wanted* him to touch her.

"What kind of answer is that? I think he would kiss her if she looked this beautiful, no matter who she belonged to. And if they stood this close. And he could smell her perfume . . . and he couldn't resist her." Daul stood close enough for Araby to see the muscle twitching in his jaw beneath his four-day beard.

"He might." Araby licked her lips, wanting, *dying* for him to kiss her.

"I wonder what it feels like to kiss another man's woman." The back of his hand brushed against a straggling curl of her blond hair, then settled on her neck. "Are you another man's woman?"

"N-no!" She shuddered involuntarily at his light touch. Were his hands always so light? She wanted to feel them on her, strong and compelling. Commanding her into his arms. Forcing her against him.

His hand slid lazily around her neck, his fingers digging into her hair. With agonizingly slow motion, his lips descended to hers, meeting them finally with a surprising softness. They tasted sweet, like cinnamon and candy apples and all the good

48

things from her childhood memories. Araby thought she couldn't get enough of his kiss, but he abruptly stepped back, breaking their languid connection.

His voice was sensuous and low. "Do you think the hero would kiss her like that, or like this?" This time Daul's lips possessed hers firmly, relaying a silent message of desire. His strong arms pulled her furiously to his muscular length, crushing her breasts against his chest and forcing their bodies together from toe to shoulder. His hand reached lower, to the small of her back, and pressed. She felt the heat of his masculinity growing stronger, hotter.

Araby soared, lost in time and space, and leaned into the kiss for more. She wanted him, wanted to know his light touch and his heavy passion. She felt the prickle of his beard against her face, but the roughness only served to increase her desire for him.

His tongue flicked over her top lip, sweet and soft and moist. His hand cupped the curve of her breast, encased in the lace and satin wedding dress, and he ran a thumb over the burgeoning nipple. She ached for his touch, longed to rip the dress away and feel his skin against hers.

Suddenly Araby realized this was more than was necessary for an improvisation of a movie scene, more than she should allow with this man who had invaded her house and her life. This man she didn't know! Things were getting out of hand!

Pressing hard against his chest, she forced them apart.

"Daul . . ."

His hand tarried for a moment longer on the softness of her breast while his eyes explored her face. Then he backed a step away, letting his hands drop to his sides. "Araby . . . sweet, soft Araby . . . I must have gotten carried away with acting out the part. But, in order to write the song, I needed to know exactly how the hero in the movie would *feel* toward his old girlfriend. You understand. It's that feeling of a man for a woman who's now taboo that I'm after. . . ."

She smoothed the bodice, physically trying to brush his lingering caress from her breast. "Well, did you find out what you needed to know? For the movie?"

"Yep." His answer was tight. "I think I know how he might feel. Maybe now I can write a song about it. You're pretty good at improvisation, Araby."

"You aren't so bad, yourself," she muttered, suddenly feeling foolish as hell for reacting so fervently to Daul's kiss. Araby wondered if these arousing feelings were make-believe or the real thing. And if he'd felt anything near the thunderbolt she did. Araby had never quite felt so heady when a man touched her, or kissed her. Certainly not from Gerry. Her breath was a little shaky as she realized how easily Daul could sweep her off her feet.

"W-Why don't you fix us a glass of tea while I

change?" she stammered, heading for the door. "Seems a little hot in here."

"Good idea." He nodded and followed her into the kitchen. When she went on into her back bedroom Daul ran a hand over his face, thinking he needed a cold shower to cool down, not merely a glass of iced tea. Damn! She did something to him! Something he couldn't control. He couldn't have stopped that kiss if he'd wanted to. And he didn't want to stop once they were together. He wanted her, completely and totally! Oh dear God, he wanted to make love with this uppity poetry professor. It was like wanting the moon!

He dumped ice cubes into the glasses and poured the tea over them. They cracked when the tepid liquid hit them, and Daul felt like he was popping inside just like those ice cubes. He had to get his head straight and forget this woman. She would be gone in a week, and he had a job to do.

Suddenly a cry of alarm came from Araby's bedroom. He rushed to the doorway, pushed the door open, then halted when he saw her. *Oh God, why is she doing this to me?*

"Daul!" She stood white-faced and stricken, wearing only panties and a bra.

"What is it?" He tried to keep his eyes on her face, away from her heaving breasts, which were falling out of that damned flimsy lace bra, and the place where her stomach sucked in below her ribs.

"Were you . . . were you just in here?"

"No, of course not. I was fixing tea," he said angrily. Dammit! Was she teasing him?

But her face revealed something different. Alarm. Bewilderment. Fear. "I heard something swishing. Something like the rustling of material, of someone moving around this room." She hugged her arms, not so much to hide her body as to warm it. "A-are you sure?"

"It must be your imagination. No one was in here but you, Araby."

"It was a sound like . . . like my aunt used to make when she rustled through a room. I thought you—someone—came in here and moved the dress."

"Your aunt? The one who lived here? Now, Araby . . ." He shook off the temptation to laugh because she was so serious. Both their gazes traveled to the wedding dress, draped over the foot of her bed.

Abruptly, Araby laughed nervously. "Oh, you're right Daul. It's nothing, just my imagination. I probably heard you dropping ice in the glasses. It's absolutely nothing! Now, will you please leave and let me finish getting dressed?"

Puzzled, Daul turned away.

Araby glanced warily around the room as if looking for something . . . or someone. Then her eyes caught on the cherry-wood heart on the dresser. Instinctively, she reached out to touch it. She lifted the lid and whispered the old-fashioned romantic words to the familiar tune:

"Let me call you sweetheart . . . I'm in love

with you. . . . Let me hear you whisper . . . that you love me too. . . . Keep the lovelight glowing in your eyes so blue. . . . Let me call you sweetheart . . . I'm in love with you."

CHAPTER THREE

Araby sat up in bed with a jolt and looked at the clock for the tenth time since midnight: 2 A.M.! This is it! I've had it! I've been patient long enough. I'm going up there and . . .

She flung off her green and gold North Carolina lily hand-quilted bedspread, grabbed her lacy white robe, and flounced out of the room. At the bottom of the attic stairs she called, "Daul, is that you making all that racket?"

The guitar strumming stopped. "Noooo . . . ooo. It's Aunt Lucyyyy," Daul taunted in a quavering voice.

"Ha! Ha!" she muttered under her breath. "I'm coming up there!" she warned and thumped heavily on every step as she climbed.

"Good." Daul played a few more bars of the tune he was inventing while he waited.

"Do you realize it's two A.M.?" She stormed into the attic, a frothy vision in white lace with angry pink cheeks.

"I do now." Daul sat smiling, obviously appreciating the feminine sight before him.

Araby stopped short when she saw him. He was clothed only in cutoff jeans! She saw a mostly bare, masculine body reclining on the colorful squares of another old-fashioned, hand-sewn quilt. His hairy legs stretched across the bright blue triangles that made up the turkey tracks design.

"Well, what do you intend to do about it?"

He shrugged. "What do you suggest? Beat the clock to a pulp?"

"How about if you clam up for the night? I'm trying to sleep!"

"I'm inspired to write," he explained, with one outstretched hand. "The mood finally struck me."

"Better the mood than me!"

"Why, Fancy Lady, I thought you came up here to inspire me," he drawled sexily.

And oh God, did he look sexy, sprawled on the bed with that guitar resting on his lap and his bare chest, muscular and bold and inviting. "Inspire you? I came here to shut you up! How the hell can anyone sleep around here with that guitar twanging away?"

"I was hoping you couldn't sleep for thinking about me, up here in this attic all alone," he murmured sweetly, then added with a growl, ". . . dying in the heat."

"Humph! I couldn't care less about you being all alone!"

"What about dying in the heat? It's hot up here, or hadn't you noticed? How can I sleep with sweat trickling down my brow? Now, maybe if you offered me your bed . . ."

"My bed?" she shrieked, appalled by his nervy suggestion.

He shrugged. "With you in it or without."

"Don't bank on it, buster!" she seethed, then silently conceded that it *was* hot. "I . . . uh, I might be able to find you a fan, though. I didn't realize it was so uncomfortable up here."

He nodded with satisfaction. "Heat rises, you know."

She ignored his innuendo and trounced down the stairs, gown tails flowing, a blond phantom with a mission. In a few minutes she returned with a small, oscillating fan. Daul sat it on an old chest of drawers and plugged it in. Immediately, it stirred the air.

"Thank God! Air! Even if it isn't very cool, it's circulating." He slumped back into his original position on the bed, leaning against the pillowed headboard. "Now, isn't that better?"

She agreed. "Why didn't you ask for a fan earlier?"

"I didn't want to disturb you." He lifted the guitar and played a G7 chord, then gazed up at her and smiled melodramatically.

Rolling her eyes, she scoffed, "So you played that whining instrument instead? I'd rather have been disturbed for a fan. Now, please go to sleep." She started to turn.

"I can't go to sleep now. I'm wide awake. Talk to me, Araby. Keep me company for a little while. Songwriting is a lonely business." He patted the turkey tracks quilt beside him in an invitation for her to join him.

"I don't see how you can do it, write, that is, any other way. That's the problem with writing. It's lonely."

"But if you keep me company, it won't be." He offered a simple solution. "Inspire me, Araby. Read your poetry to me."

Her eyes caught his, and she felt their soft gray seductiveness, their appealing warmth. She was sinking into their depths fast. "Read it aloud? No, I'd rather not." She edged along the wall toward the stairs, feeling like the fly about to be caught in the spider's web.

"Why? We're both writers, subject to the same kinds of frustrations. And rejections."

Her eyes narrowed. What did he know of rejection? His work had been published!

He continued. "I know what you're thinking. I can see it in your expression. You think I don't get rejected anymore, don't you? You think that just because some of my songs have been published, they snap up everything I write. Wrong! Would you believe that I have a trunk full of songs? Rejected and unpublished!"

"I . . . I guess I never thought of it that way, Daul."

He shrugged. "I'm a writer, like you, Araby. I promise I won't be judgmental of your work. Please read it. It might inspire me. Wouldn't you like to have a hand in helping a former student write a hit song?"

"Former student! That's a laugh. I don't know what you were doing in my poetry class that night, but you certainly didn't belong there. I'm the one who should be taking lessons from you. Um, on how to write for publication."

"I was learning the importance of a single word, the value of pacing, and all about iambic pentameter rhythm from a certain beautiful lady professor who doesn't look old enough to hold the uppity title of doctor. Come on, Professor," he encouraged with a slow smile. "Put me in the mood to write a love song."

"You're very persuasive," she hedged. "I've never done anything like this before."

"I hope I'm convincing. I need your help, Araby."

"I . . . oh, hell. Okay. If you promise not to laugh."

He raised his right hand with a solemn "I promise."

The white apparition in gossamer and lace disappeared down the stairs a second time. She returned with several wrinkled sheets of paper clutched nervously in her hands and stood at the foot of the iron bedstead.

Again he patted the blue turkey tracks. "Get comfortable. Have a seat, Araby."

With a weak glance around the room, Araby realized there was no place to sit but on the bed. Unless she wanted to sit on the dusty floor or a box. Araby gaped at the old-fashioned bed with decorative, white-iron head and foot rails. Although it was a bed designed for two, she remembered Aunt Lucy having to order the mattress special-made because it was narrower than modern double beds. As she carefully sat down on the near edge of the bed she thought it looked very narrow indeed.

Araby cleared her throat and began to read in a low, slightly shaky voice. It was the first time anyone else had heard her poems, except a few nameless editors who obviously didn't appreciate them.

Daul listened quietly, his dark, devil's eyes hooded and almost closed.

When she finished the first one she paused for a moment and took a deep breath. Reading her own poetry aloud, laying her feelings bare like that, was nerve-racking. Her blue eyes crept up to meet Daul's. Suddenly she felt like a child, a twenty-nine-year-old child seeking approval.

His expression was more professional than she expected. He was not going to fawn all over the place about her work. Nor was he going to destroy it. His eyes narrowed, as if he were deep in thought. "Lovely, Araby. Very good, in fact. Do you have anything about love? This movie deals with several kinds of love, and the songs must reflect that . . . that special feeling."

She was extremely relieved. They were dealing with a different aspect of writing, a step above the emotional. He was looking for a specific idea, a certain feeling. And he was being true to his word. Not judgmental. The poem was neither outstandingly wonderful nor ridiculously awful. Just, does it work?

"Well, this one," Araby conceded with a light chuckle. "But it's too . . ." She caught herself short. She almost said it. Almost repeated what that insensitive editor had said about it in the rejection letter.

"Yes?" Daul waited, an expectant half-smile on his lips.

She gave an embarrassed little laugh. "The last editor called it 'too schmaltzy.'"

"Hmmm. Sounds like it might fit right in with this movie. Read me the schmaltzy one." He was serious.

She hesitated, then read. Midway through the first verse, Daul unconsciously strummed a chord on the guitar. Araby stopped reading and looked up. Was that about all he could take of the schmaltzy one?

He played the chord again. "'Searching for a place in your heart . . .'" He sang her last line in a low, sensitive voice. "Beautiful. Don't stop. Go on."

She took a deep breath and continued. "'Though our parting, set our souls free, in the end, love is all that matters to me.'"

"Araby, that's beautiful."

"But, schmaltzy."

"Wrong. Sensitive. Touching. Full of love."

Using her finger, she traced the turkey track design near her knee. She couldn't help it. She was still on the emotional level with her poems. "I wrote this after Aunt Lucy died. She meant so much to me I wanted to express my love for her in

60

some kind of tribute. She inspired me. And encouraged me. I felt our spirits were entwined somehow. So, actually, the love in this poem is for someone very dear, but not necessarily of a woman for a man."

"But it could apply." Daul laid the guitar aside.

"Oh?" She felt rather than saw him move toward her.

"The words. They could apply to a man's love for a woman. Or hers for him."

"Yes, I suppose so. You mean, for the movie?"

"For anyone." His hands gripped her arms, pulling her toward him. "Do you believe the words, Araby? That in the end, love is all that matters?"

"Yes," she whispered feebly. She was weak, unable to resist him, not even wanting to. "Do you?" Araby lifted her arms, and her hands came in hard contact with his bare ribs. She felt his trembling reaction to her touch as she clung to him, helpless in his grasp.

"I believe that right now love is all that matters. What's happening between us is all that counts. Oh, Araby . . ." His lips caressed hers in feather-soft strokes, teasing them open, then sealing them with his own.

At that moment Daul's desire for her was complete and compelling. The curious urge that had begun at a simple poetry class could be sated tonight. Oh yes, he wanted her more than he'd wanted a woman in a long time. She had been elusive, unattainable until tonight. With a growing strength, he gathered her to him, his hard thighs on either side of her, drawing her up against the power of his body.

Araby could feel the heat of his passion, the electric force that was transmitted from his body to hers. With an inner rushing of fevered emotions, she shared his heated passion. She reached out and slid her hands around his bare back, then felt her way up the rivulets of muscles, thrilling to every hot inch of him. She longed for the sizzle of his body against hers.

Araby arched upward, surging to meet Daul's energy, to match it. Swirling. Reaching. They were swept together on the bed, warm lips to warm lips, heated body to heated body. Araby wasn't sure when, or how, but they were soon lying on the bed, she writhing joyously beneath him.

Daul's gray eyes were smoky-dark with passion as he hovered over her, kissing, teasing, savoring. Araby's blond hair spread across the blue turkey tracks quilt, her mouth smiling sensuously as she seductively invited each kiss. Daul trailed kisses from her crimson lips down her neck to the wildly pulsing spot on her neck. He wondered if her nipples were as pink as her lips, and suddenly he longed to see them.

They were becoming entangled in the white lace, fevered hands groping through slippery folds of material. Impatiently he shoved at the lace and sought her heaving breast with eager lips. One hand cupped and caressed while his lips placed heated kisses along the other gentle swell. He pinched the tip gently between thumb and fore-finger while his lips set her skin afire with aching passion. She moaned in a low, kittenish tone as he continued to excite her.

"You're soft and inviting, sweet Araby," he murmured, switching his lips to the other breast. "So soft, I want to bury myself in you."

She arched beneath him, lifting her breasts erotically to meet his magnificent touch.

"Are you this soft everywhere?" His legs straddled hers as his hands framed her sides and followed her shape down past her waist to the feminine curve of her hips. His hands seemed lost in that filmy gown and lacy white robe as he pressed inward, stretching his thumbs to the center of her desire. They stroked her, sending spirals of desire shooting in all directions. "Do you want me, Araby?"

"Yes, yes . . ." She was wild for his touch, begging for his passion, for his fulfillment.

His hands somehow found their way under her nightgown and grasped her knees, sliding upward along the silken flesh of her inner thighs.

"Oh, Daul . . ." Araby moved and shifted beneath him.

God, he wanted her, wanted her now. And she wanted him. Her actions told him that.

"Araby," he groaned. "This gown has to go . . ."

He shifted so they could remove the garments—and everything happened at once. The bloodcurdling yowl. The thump as something landed on the bed. Araby's scream.

She pushed Daul aside and struggled to get up. "What is that? Someone's in here! Who is it?" The strange, unexplained noises in her bedroom that afternoon had already made her edgy. Now she was hearing them again!

"It's just the cat," he groaned, knowing the moment of passion had been completely destroyed.

She jerked her lacy robe back onto her shoulders. "What cat?"

"Araby!" He lay back on the turkey tracks quilt with a low groan.

"I . . . we can't let this happen, Daul. It's too soon, and just not right and . . . and we're not . . . we're too different."

"You can't do this!" Daul muttered furiously. "Can't just stop like this! Don't you know—"

"I know perfectly well, Daul. But this isn't right, and you know it. We were about to give in to lust to satisfy our sexual desires." She slipped from his grasp and tried to pull the gown down over her thighs before she rose from the bed.

"So what's wrong with that?"

She shook her head, now embarrassed by her own behavior. "I'm no prude, Daul, but I don't just go hopping into bed with anyone who can give me pleasure."

"You wanted me, too, Araby."

"Yes, but, thank God, it was a fleeting desire." She was on her feet, straightening her gown.

Immediately, Daul was beside her, gripping her

shoulders tightly. "Don't you ever do that to me again, Fancy Lady. The next time you lead me on, nothing will stop me. I never was much of a gentleman anyway, and I'll forget you were ever a lady. It'll be man against woman. And I'll win."

"Are you threatening me?" she asked angrily.

He shoved her aside. "Take it any way you want to. But don't you dare tease me like that again."

"I didn't . . . I didn't start this."

"You came up here in the first place!"

"But for different reasons!"

"Think about it, Araby! Just why did you come up those stairs the second time?"

"The fan . . ." she said weakly.

"Well, the third time, then! You made three trips up here tonight! Three times you paraded around in that revealing lacy robe! And you expect me to ignore you? I'm not made of steel!"

She looked down. He was right. She came, not to read her poetry, but because she wanted to be with him. At that moment her eyes caught the switching tail of the intrusive cat, and she chose to change the subject. "Where did that cat come from?"

"The calico, from the barn."

"That stray? Well, get him out of my house."

"*She* stays," Daul said pointedly. "There are mice in this attic, and she's an excellent mouser."

"What? Mice in this house?" Araby was appalled. "Ridiculous! Aunt Lucy has never had mice!"

"Well, she sure has them now. They are rampant

in this attic. And I'm not sleeping in a place where mice can nibble at my feet. Or anything else!"

Araby eyed the multicolored cat, who was investigating Daul's bare feet. "I have never lived with an animal in my house, and I don't intend to start now. I want this one out immediately."

"Would you rather have the mice? Or the cat?"

"Set a mouse trap," was her easy solution. "The cat goes."

"The cat stays," he countered in a commanding voice. "You, however, may go any time you please, Fancy Lady."

"Just who the hell do you think you are, Daul McNeal? You come into my house and think you can take over! You keep me awake nights with your lousy guitar music, move cats into the house and let them roam all night, then have the nerve to throw me out of my own place!"

"Cat, singular. And this is my place. I merely invited you to leave. Since I'm renting this space for the month, it's mine! There was nothing in the contract that prohibited pets."

She folded her arms. "There was no contract. It's still *my* house and it's against *my* policy to have animals in it."

He folded his arms, too, and met her nose to nose. "Money was exchanged. We made a binding, verbal agreement. This is *my* attic for the month. I rest my case. Out, Fancy Lady! And leave *my* cat alone."

With a loud harrumph and with her nose in the

air, Araby flounced back down the stairs, clutching her precious sheets of poetry.

She paced the floor of her bedroom and kicked a couple of chairs out of her way. Finally, after working herself into a fine lather, Araby grabbed her *Writer's Market.* Her finger slid past the checked and crossed-through names of publishers.

There's one I haven't sent to. It pays in copies, she read. Damn. Oh, well, it's better than nothing. Not much, but at least I would get them published and have copies to hand out to all my colleagues.

What was this crazy urge to see her work in print? She didn't even bother to answer her own question, but addressed the manila envelope to yet another university press. The poems would go out tomorrow for sure.

The next morning Araby was still fuming over the events of the night before when Daul strode lazily down the stairs.

"I've been thinking, Araby." He edged around the two boxes she was packing in the middle of the kitchen and poured himself a cup of coffee.

"That's an interesting pastime," she snipped.

"So have I. And I want to apologize for my behavior. You were right. I'll take the blame, but believe me, it won't happen again."

Daul raised one eyebrow. *Won't happen again, sweet Araby? Don't bank on it! I've already had a taste of you, and I won't stop now until I've savored the entire meal!* He ignored her apology and continued in a normal tone. "What if we combined forces and wrote a song together? Lots of people have done it. We'd use your poetry as lyrics, and my music. Put them together and— pow! A hit song!"

She stood up and looked at him curiously. Wiping her dusty hands on her hips, she then rested her fingers inside the rear pockets of her jeans, pondering his proposal. "Use my poetry in your country songs?"

"Yep."

"*My* words—sung? Surely you jest!" Her eyes snapped as they suddenly lit with blue fire.

"No," he said quietly. "I'm very serious—"

"Well, forget it! No country bumpkin is going to sing my words to the tune of a fiddle!"

"What if we call it a violin?" Daul offered tolerantly, with a wry smile.

"Country is country is country!" she fired.

"And stubborn is stubborn is stubborn!" he countered. "Let me tell you something, Fancy Lady. More people will hear your precious words in a country-music song than will ever read them in some higher-than-thou literary publication. Unless you're just doing this to impress a limited number of narrow-minded people!"

"Narrow-minded?" she sputtered, immediately thinking of B. Nettington Goodfield, with his reams of published poetry, and Gerrald Hughes, her accountant boyfriend. How would she tell them that she'd sold her soul to country music? "It just isn't something I would consider doing. I appreciate your offer, Daul, but no thanks. Anyway,

I've already mailed them off to another publisher."

"Well, go out to the mailbox and retrieve them!" Daul gestured toward the door. "The mailman doesn't come until late afternoon."

"No."

He examined her closely, his steel-gray eyes cutting into her. "You're turning down a chance to sell your poetry to a songwriter? I know of people who would beg or fight for an opportunity like this. Do you know how much money you could make?"

"Money isn't everything, Daul."

"Neither is high-handed stubbornness, Fancy Lady." He turned and walked way.

Araby finished packing the box and taped the top together securely. Later she checked the mailbox, just to see if the mailman had come.

CHAPTER FOUR

Araby did a lot of thinking about Daul's hotly spoken words during the next two days. He just didn't understand her desire to get published or her personal aspirations. Apparently his aspirations were radically different from hers. He sought public acclaim and financial rewards. She was looking for more esoteric satisfaction.

She was a professor first, a researcher. She delved into the past, honed in on certain areas such as Emily Dickinson's life and work and studied and evaluated them. She took pride in this work. Her own drive to write was a labor of love that emanated from a strong desire to share her deepest feelings with others and to make an important contribution to society.

Her work wasn't meant for the masses, as was Daul's. Her message was much more serious than his "lost-my-woman blues" songs. Her work wasn't dependent on someone else's story. No movie producer was telling her what to write. Ugh! she shuddered. Her poetry sprung from her own personal experience, as Emily Dickinson's had. It was only natural to want to publish her work so she could share it with other people.

But she had to admit the strong obligation she felt to publish was prompted by her department head, Dr. B. Nettington Goodfield. "You know, Araby, you would establish yourself as a serious teacher in this English department if you'd get yourself published. It would enhance your educational professionalism," he had said.

She interpreted that as meaning "You'll be rewarded, both financially and principally, if you publish."

Behind his back, everyone referred to Dr. Goodfield as "Nettie." But to his face people used his formal title. After Nettie's well-spoken advice, Araby had begun to consider some of the outpourings of her heart as perhaps being of publishable quality. She sought specialized, elite publications where readers would experience great insight, feel deep emotions, quietly appreciate the merits of the writer.

How utterly gauche to have your innermost feelings sung to the tune of a guitar in a smoke-filled room!

Araby sighed and looked around the bare walls of the living room. "Well, Aunt Lucy," she mumbled, half to herself. "This is the last of the knick-knacks. I've saved some of the family pictures. And I couldn't bear to part with the wooden music box. But the rest of this stuff will have to go to charity. I thought I'd call the Baptist preacher today."

"Did I hear something about a preacher? Think he might disapprove of our living arrangement?"

Araby whirled around at the sound of Daul's voice responding to her mumblings. "Were you eavesdropping?" she asked.

He shrugged with a half-grin. "I just walked up this minute and heard you talking."

"I'll bet! You've probably been standing there half an hour."

"I have more important things to do than stand around and listen to you talk to yourself. I came here to work, remember?"

"Oh yes. You're the one writing love songs."

"It beats talking to yourself."

"I wasn't—" She halted mid-sentence. Then *who* was she talking to?

Daul didn't ask the inevitable question, though. He just looked at her with the strangest expression on his face, as if he were reading her mind.

They had carefully avoided each other for two laborious days, with Daul eating out and Araby fixing a sandwich or nibbling a boiled egg at odd hours. Normal working hours became reversed, with Daul sleeping most of the day and Araby trying to catch a few winks at night in spite of the distant twangs of guitar music.

As they stood facing each other for the first time in two days, the anger of their earlier confrontations was momentarily forgotten. Almost tangible between them were memories of soft touches, electric kisses, endearing words. In the magnetic attraction of man for woman, they were caught, spellbound, unable to move.

"Araby . . ." Daul's voice was low and gruff, and he wore the offensive shirt that so blatantly stated his philosophy.

"Yes?" She glanced up at him, her blond hair drawn back in a blue ribbon at her nape, her cotton blouse streaked with dirt and sweat. The jeans were no longer sharply creased, but sprung at the knees from kneeling so much. In short, she looked a mess. And that was something that rarely happened.

"Araby, the garden is a wreck," he blurted, his gray eyes darkening seriously.

"What?" She stared, startled by his statement. Who the hell cared about the garden? She expected a confession or, at least, an apology over their disagreements. Instead she was getting the farm report.

"The vegetable garden out back." He gestured. "It's infested with weeds and half eaten by rabbits. But there are a few vegetables left. I think I can salvage them. Is it okay with you?"

Araby shrugged and almost laughed with the intensity of the conversation over a few dying plants. "I don't care. Mr. Gosset used the garden all summer, but I'm sure he's finished with it. I thought it was all dead by now."

"Not quite." Daul smiled tightly. He started to turn, but stopped to give her a delightful wink. "I'll fix you a great Southern meal straight from the garden tonight," he promised, then was gone.

Araby opened her mouth to say "Don't bother." But the back door slammed, and she stood staring at the empty space where he'd been. Daul had actually winked at her, like they were good ole buddies! "He acts as if a good meal will solve everything," she grunted softly as she shoved the packed box against the wall.

Sitting on top of the box, she rested her left ankle on her right knee and recalled how Aunt Lucy always joked that the way to a man's heart was through his stomach. And, oh Jiminy, how her aunt could cook! "Apparently, he believes your philosophy about the heart being near the stomach, Aunt Lucy. He thinks I'm that gullible," she grumbled. "Hell, it's just like him to be thinking of his stomach! He's probably tired of eating out. Or eating alone." *Or sleeping alone!* . . . Well, he could dig in the garden and think of food to his heart's content.

Araby stuffed her hands into her jeans pockets, sauntered to the kitchen window, and absently watched Daul hack away at the remains of the weedy garden. He had removed his shirt, and she couldn't help but marvel at the width of his shoulders and the sleekness of his waist. The well-developed muscular definitions of his arms and back shimmered with perspiration, and the sun reflected a multipointed diamond of light on his shiny black hair.

Caught up in the sight of him, Araby watched him work for a while, privately admiring his sinewy body bending under the sun, his skin glistening with the glow of hard work. She wondered why he did it. Why did he bother, when it wasn't even his garden, when he wouldn't ever use it again? But the farmer in him persisted for a greater part of the afternoon as he cleaned out the dead corn stalks and drooping tomato plants.

She had to admit there was something admirable in a man who labored, who bent his back to work the land. Araby mused that it must be her distant roots, her long-forgotten elemental self that harkened to this admiration of a man who worked so hard and wiped a sweaty brow. For some strange reason he appealed to her more than a man who sat behind a desk and pushed a pencil or, worse yet, a man who hunched behind a guitar and made up songs about loving and losing!

When Daul headed toward the house with an odd assortment of the fruits of his labor, Araby quickly pretended to be busy. She didn't even look up when he placed his treasures on the counter beside the sink. Red and green tomatoes. Several stunted ears of corn. A handful of okra. A couple of zucchini.

"Hope you haven't packed away the cast-iron skillet," he said seriously. "It's the best pan for making corn bread. And I've got my eye on some wild poke greens behind the barn. It'll be great with corn bread."

"Corn bread?" Araby sputtered, casting a glance at the vegetables, then a roving eye over his bare, still-glistening torso. "Now listen here, Daul, I'm not—"

"Who's asking you to fix it?" he interrupted, knowing instinctively what she was about to say. "I'll do it. I've been doing most of the cooking around here anyway. Why should we change the routine now? Tonight you're invited to partake of a good, ole down-home country supper. Nobody's asking you to do a thing but eat it."

"Routine? We—you haven't been here long enough to develop a routine." Araby watched him head for the back door. "This is ridiculous, Daul McNeal! If you think you can make amends for your rudeness by preparing a meal for me, you're crazy! I don't even care about—"

He wheeled around to face her, an expression of dead seriousness on his face. "This isn't going to be just *any* meal, Araby. It'll be an old-fashioned, Southern dinner, straight from Aunt Lucy's garden. Perhaps it'll be the last time you'll ever eat a bite of food that comes from this soil. There is something very special about that."

"Special? To whom? You? It isn't even your garden! If you think this . . . this stupid meal is going to change my opinion of you, you're nuts. I don't give a damn about your Southern cooking because your Southern manners are despicable!"

"Well." He grinned devilishly and hooked his thumbs in the empty belt loops of his jeans. The snug, faded jeans hung low on his hips and the additional weight of his hands tugged them well below his navel. "Wouldn't you like to tackle the job of teaching me some decent manners, Fancy Lady?"

She forced her eyes from the dark trail of hair that disappeared beneath the snap on his jeans. "No, I—"

Before Araby could step back, his hands had clasped her wrists, pulling her dangerously close to him. Daul lowered his face to within inches of hers and she watched the movement of his lips behind the dark beard.

"Araby, come down off that high horse of yours and I'll teach you more than Southern manners. I think you'll enjoy it more than anything you could ever imagine!"

"You're crude, Daul McNeal!"

They were dizzyingly close. He breathed fire onto her lips, his eyes burned with undisguised passion, his body heat radiated against her. Daul was sweaty from his work in the garden, and Araby found his strong, earthy scent arousing. She tried not to get caught in the depths of his smoky gray eyes, tried not to feel their gaze penetrating to her very core. She wanted to resist him, to despise him, but the inexorable hurricane of sensuality that surrounded him swept her toward him. And in that moment she desired him. It was a sweeping desire that gushed through her, leaving her feeling weak and close to tears.

Her only defense was her sharp tongue. "You couldn't teach me anything, you country bumpkin!"

He grinned maddeningly, his white teeth gleaming against his black beard. "I could teach you about good, old-fashioned passion and the joys of desire . . ." He let the last words trail off to a whisper. "Come on, Araby. Soften up that hard shell you've built around yourself. Let a little fun slip into your life."

"We have absolutely nothing in common, Daul McNeal. Especially not passion!"

"How would you know? I don't think you've ever experienced it!"

"You don't know what I've experienced."

"You haven't experienced this." He drew her against him with the suddenness of a bird of prey, her lips captured by his, her body forced against his. She gasped as his tongue found entry between her lips and plunged immediately to a deeper sweetness. The pulsating motion entering her mouth drew a small, guttural moan from her and she felt the restraint leave her body, against her protesting will. She wanted to fight him away, but her body betrayed her. She couldn't move away from him.

Daul pushed her back against the refrigerator, its coolness contrasting with the flames that licked along the front part of her body, the part that stayed in contact with Daul. His lips would not let go; his hands cupped each breast with caressing fingers; his knee forced itself between her thighs. The stroking, the caressing, the pressure drove her wild, and the more Araby struggled against him, the more inflamed she became.

He held her firmly, refusing to release her until he'd quenched his thirst for her sweetness. Daul's skillful fingers unbuttoned her blouse, freeing her heaving breasts and revealing her bra-less state. His lips abandoned hers immediately to kiss each throbbing, swelling breast.

Araby used the moment to bombard him. "You . . . you bastard!" She shoved impotently at his shoulders.

"Take it easy, Araby, and enjoy," Daul murmured vibrantly from inside her blouse where his lips caressed each bare, creamy mound.

"Ohhh," she protested, feeling the intensely pleasurable sensations he was evoking in her. "No! No, don't!"

His tongue circled the enlarged tip, bringing it to an aching tautness. "Oh yes, Araby, you're enjoying this. See how your body reacts?"

Her breasts heaved and responded to his touch in spite of her protests. Unavoidably, they rose to thrust against his teeth. "Are you . . ." She struggled to speak coherently. "Are you going to rape me this time?"

"Rape is not my style. I think you want me Araby . . . admit it." His kisses trailed fire back up her arched neck to her parted lips.

She wrenched away. "I would never want you, you . . . despicable hayseed!"

He lifted his head and dark, angry eyes glared at her. Instantly she feared him and regretted her heedlessly spoken words. Fear, however, prevented her from speaking. She just stared at him with blue eyes wide and her blouse hanging open.

He roughly shoved her away. "You are so tight-assed, you probably wouldn't know what a climax was if you ever had one, which I doubt!"

"Get out of this kitchen! Get out of my house!"

He laughed tauntingly at her anger. "Can't do that, Araby. Not yet. Aunt Lucy and I have a deal! I'll get you, yet!"

Araby's hand closed over the nearest object on the kitchen cabinet and hurled it at Daul with all her might. The tan crockery bowl crashed into a million pieces against the back door, and Daul's laughter could be heard as he escaped to the yard.

Oh, how she hated him! Araby rushed over and knelt to pick up the largest of the pot chards. Some of the pieces were big enough to see the blue and brown stripes that encircled the old bowl. It was Aunt Lucy's favorite for mixing cakes and . . . corn bread. Now, because of Daul, it was gone forever. Oh, who the hell cares about a bowl? It was chipped, anyway. Araby grabbed a broom and began to sweep furiously, tears welling in her deep blue eyes as she tried to tell herself that she didn't care about any cheap old bowl. But she knew it wasn't the broken bowl that disturbed her. It was Daul McNeal.

Later Araby tried to ignore the lighthearted whistling coming from the direction of the kitchen. She glared at the closed door of her bedroom. How could he continue with this charade? She had no intention of eating with him tonight. The bridge had been blown apart, and now the gulf between them was wider than ever.

Now that she could think straight, she wondered what in hell he meant by the remark that he and Aunt Lucy had a deal. The idea was absurd! Surely he had never known Aunt Lucy, had he? Then what kind of deal could they have? It was ridiculous!

Her eyes rested on the music box and she caressed its smooth surface. Her thumb flicked the top up, setting off the tiny mechanics inside. . . . *in your eyes so blue. . . . Let me call you—* Araby slammed the heart-shaped lid down.

Try as she might, Araby couldn't obliterate the sounds and marvelous aromas coming from the kitchen, right next to her bedroom. She flounced on the green- and gold-quilted bed, studying the intricate handwork beneath her. Just as Araby decided that her best course of action would be to finish packing and get away from the farmhouse— and Daul McNeal—as soon as possible, a tentative knock interrupted her thoughts.

How dare he, she thought arrogantly, jerking the door open. "What do you want this time?"

"Do you accept apologies? And small glasses of vino?" He extended his hand.

Although she wanted to perpetuate her anger until the very moment she stomped out of the house, something about his effort and the sincerity in his gray eyes wore down her reserve. She accepted the crystal goblet from him and raised her eyes to his, a mistake she would later realize was fatal.

Daul bowed formally, a comical gesture in itself since he was clad in jeans and the familiar old plaid

81

shirt. It had that fresh, dried-on-the-line smell and was unmercifully wrinkled as it stretched across his wide-angled shoulders. "M' lady, please accept my apology for my boorish behavior earlier in the day. It is no excuse, but it is a fact that your beauty tears me apart inside, leaving me with no ability to restrain myself. I promise not to touch you again, unless you ask, of course."

Araby stared at him for a long moment, trying to remain angry, struggling to forget the heated flush that had engulfed her body for a full hour after he'd gone back to his gardening. She smiled weakly. "Apology accepted. And don't hold your breath to be asked."

He clicked his goblet to hers and the crystal emitted a high, clear note. "As you wish, m' lady. But, may I remind you what you're missing—"

"I don't care what I'm missing! Why don't you stop while you're ahead?"

"Who said I was ahead? You still look pretty dour to me. What you need, I think, is a good, old-fashioned, home-cooked meal. Complete with corn bread. Dinner will be served in about fifteen minutes and your lovely presence is heartily desired." He wheeled around and headed back into the kitchen.

Araby sipped her wine and closed her door. And smiled. In spite of being extremely angry with the man, perturbed beyond endurance, exasperated by his unceasing activities, and unnerved by his masculinity, she smiled. And why not? She'd have to be a brass-plated robot not to find him appealing. He was no longer—what had she called him—a country bumpkin? Oh Lord, how rude of her!

When he'd come to her door he'd smelled fresh and clean and . . . spicy. He must have used a dab of cologne after his shower. Also, Daul had been polite. How could she refuse his dinner offer? After all, it was her kitchen, the food grown in her garden. And this would be the last time she would eat anything grown in this sacred Tennessee soil. Besides, she was starved!

Araby didn't wait the fifteen minutes to join Daul in the kitchen. "My, my, your manners have improved drastically since the heat of the afternoon," she declared breezily, reminding herself that she probably owed him an apology too.

"It's amazing what good breeding will produce," he answered saucily, stirring the contents of the skillet. "Breeding and mingling with the upper class. You'll notice I even changed clothes for m' lady."

"A great improvement, I have to admit. Even the air's sweeter." How could she apologize when he wouldn't give her a chance?

"But, you must remember, the basic core of the man is still the same." He checked the bread baking in the oven. "Country bumpkin, through and through."

She moved closer, a contrite expression on her face. "Daul, I should apologize, too, for the things I said. I didn't really mean them. I was just so angry. I shouldn't have thrown that hayseed comment at

83

you. After all, I'm country-bred too. The same standards apply to me."

He turned around to give her a blatant once-over. "I'd hardly call you 'country.' Classy, maybe."

"Our roots are similar." She smiled softly, then added, "Why, I even know what poke salad is. And how good it is with corn bread. Doesn't it take a real country girl to know that?"

"Yeah, I guess so." He turned back to the skillet. "Does a real country girl like fried okra?"

"Love it! And what's this? Fried green tomatoes?" She poked her nose curiously around his elbow. "Oh, Daul, I haven't had fried green tomatoes in . . . in a coon's age!"

"What?" he laughed. "I haven't heard that expression since I left the Arkansas farm!"

"Believe me, I haven't used that expression since I left *this* farm." She popped a browned okra nugget into her mouth. "Aunt Lucy used to make them exactly like this."

"Oh? Thin-sliced and dipped in milk, then corn meal?"

"Yep. She said it makes the best batter for frying vegetables."

He opened the oven and drew out the black cast-iron skillet. The distinctive aroma of fresh-baked corn bread filled the kitchen. "Ahh, nice," he approved with relish. "My compliments to the chef!"

"Hmmmm, smells wonderful!" Araby watched as Daul turned the round, crusty bread upside down on the serving plate. "How do you get it so crunchy on the outside?"

"Secret's in the pan." He gave the bread a satisfied look. "You have to get the well-greased pan good and hot before you pour in the batter. That's why you use a cast-iron skillet. It holds and distributes the heat best. When you pour in your cornbread batter, it sizzles and starts to cook right away."

"I feel as though I've just had a cooking lesson from Aunt Lucy. These are things she prepared regularly."

"Sounds as though she was a good cook." Daul took up the last of the fried green tomatoes and placed them beside the corn bread and black-eyed peas on the table. "Ready to eat?"

Araby nodded eagerly and the two of them began to butter wedges of corn bread and apply a dash of vinegar to the cooked poke salad greens. "I know this sounds crazy, Daul, but all of this reminds me so much of Aunt Lucy, it's almost as though she's here. I mean, she could have fixed this very meal! It brings back so many memories. . . ."

Daul watched Araby's expression for a moment and realized that she was slightly disturbed. "Maybe it's because you've been packing her things and thinking about her a lot lately. It reminds you that she was once so much a part of the life here on the farm."

"You're probably right." Araby popped several nuggets of fried okra into her mouth and murmured slowly, "I've tried to get her out of my mind, but today she just won't leave me alone." Araby halted and looked up with a start. "Oh, my God, that's nonsense! How stupid of me to say that! Of course, she can't—"

"Araby, it isn't stupid. It's possible."

"Oh no, it isn't! I don't believe in anything I can't see, Daul. I'm a realistic, logical person. There's no such thing as ghosts." With a definitive motion of her fork, Araby took a bite of fried tomato.

Daul mulled the subject quietly for a few minutes. "I'm not sure I completely agree with you, Araby. I have a feeling for this Aunt Lucy I've never met. Maybe it's just because I'm living in her home."

Araby leaned forward with a smile. "To be perfectly honest, I think Aunt Lucy would have liked you, Daul. She would love your crazy sense of humor as well as your songwriting career. She probably would have been delighted to contribute to it in some way. Maybe by playing the banjo as accompaniment or something."

"Ah, a musician. A woman after my own heart. She played the banjo?"

Araby angled her head to give a slight nod. "Sometimes. If the occasion was right."

"She sounds like a very interesting woman. Tell me more about this lady whose home I've invaded, and whose spirit still pervades these walls."

"Spirit?" Araby looked at him, aghast. "Do you . . . do you really believe that, Daul?"

His hand slid reassuringly over hers. "Well, doesn't she?"

"I . . . I guess so." Araby glanced uneasily around the room. "It's eerie to imagine Aunt Lucy's spirit being around here, when I know she's been gone for years."

Daul shrugged. "There's nothing wrong with that. After all, this was her place. What was the dear lady like?"

As they ate, Araby talked about her aunt. The words came surprisingly easy, and for the first time unemotionally. "Aunt Lucy was a character, all right. Interesting. Unusual. Lovable. She smoked an occasional cheroot. Said she had to continue Uncle John's tradition. But I know it was because she liked doing it. She never did anything she didn't want to do.

"She was a widow for most of her life that I remember. That doesn't mean she was without suitors. But she never remarried. One summer, though, a man from Atlanta spent several weeks here with Aunt Lucy. She was very discreet about the situation and said he was here to make repairs on the barn roof. But I suspect they were lovers, because the roof continued to leak."

"Then she wouldn't frown on our present living arrangement?" Daul proposed with a sly smile.

"Oh, heavens no! Of course, there's nothing going on here to invite her disapproval," Araby observed. "Aunt Lucy was nonjudgmental, a rarity in these parts. One time I remember she took in a young, pregnant girl who was unmarried. She kept her here until the baby was about six months old and the girl could get a job and make living arrangements in Nashville. That was a very avant-garde thing to do in those days. But, you know, the girl always stayed in touch, and my aunt kept pictures of that child as she grew up. They are still in the family album. I met them, the mother and her grown daughter . . . at Aunt Lucy's funeral."

"She sounds like a remarkable woman. Someone I'd like to meet."

Araby patted her palms on the table. "Well, I know what Aunt Lucy would say now. 'This messy kitchen won't clean itself!' "

She and Daul worked together to wash and dry the dishes. It was a comfortable task after a satisfying meal.

"The country supper was delicious, Daul. Thanks." Araby smiled sincerely. "It brought back lots of wonderful memories." Maybe it *was* the way to her heart. What a sucker she was for schmaltz, she thought.

"Let's sit on the front porch for a little while. Isn't that what they used to do on the farm? Sit on the front porch and swing after supper?" His firm hand on her shoulder led her outside.

Araby laughed. "Not Aunt Lucy. She was always going somewhere. The Grand Ole Opry in Nashville was one of her favorites. And she even frequented Printer's Alley."

"Ahhh, Nashville's den of iniquity!" Daul chuckled as he avoided the porch swing and sat in the wooden rocker instead. "The more I hear about this lady, the more I like her."

Araby chose the cane-bottom chair and sat watching summer fireflies flashing in the darkness. "We called them lightning bugs," she said finally.

"So did we," Daul agreed, his image outlined by the faint glow of a quarter moon. "Did you ever catch a June bug?"

"Those green, iridescent things? Oh yes." Araby laughed low, shuddering with the memory. "And let it crawl over your hands?"

"And tie a string around one leg and let it fly in circles?"

"Boys can be so cruel! My cousin, Jimmy Darrel, did it, partly to aggravate me." She sighed. "Then Aunt Lucy would make peach ice cream. It was marvelous on a hot summer night with lumps of icy peaches . . ."

"There are some fond memories associated with this place, aren't there, Araby?" His voice was a calming tone in the dark.

"Yes," she admitted soberly. "That's why it's been so difficult for me to pack everything away. It means the end of an era, and I guess I'm reluctant to close it."

"That's normal, you know."

"Yeah, I guess. I have my emotions under control now, though. There are certain things I'll keep. But most of it will have to go. I called a local minister today, and he knows several families in the area who can use these things. He's bringing a pickup truck tomorrow. Will you help him load the truck, Daul?"

"Sure."

"I want everything in the attic to go, except for the iron bed, of course."

"Thank goodness," Daul quipped. "For a minute there, I thought the cat and I'd be curled up on the floor together."

"Do you still have that . . . that cat?" Araby had forgotten about the creature in light of their other arguments.

"Who, Mama-cat? Sure do. Best lil' mouser in the country!"

"Mama-cat? Does that mean—"

"Yep. She's pregnant."

"Oh, my God, Daul! You just have to get that animal out of the house! I should have known! We do not need a litter of kittens around here!"

"Just think of it as doing a creature a good turn. After all, Aunt Lucy couldn't turn away the pregnant girl who needed her help."

"But that was different! This is—oh, you just don't understand, do you?"

"Not quite. Anyway, you'll be gone soon, so it's not your worry."

"You're right," she confirmed. "I'm leaving in a couple of days. The furniture goes tomorrow. Also, Mr. Calhoun, another farmer who lives down the road, is coming for the hay. And he knows someone who might buy the tractor and other farm implements."

"Sounds as if you almost have it wrapped up."

"Yes. I think Aunt Lucy'd approve of—well, I mean, she always wanted to help people and . . ."

Daul picked up on her strangulated words. "You're following Aunt Lucy's advice?"

Araby reacted sharply. "Of course not! I'm doing what I think is right. It's my decision."

"Don't you think Aunt Lucy's spirit might be guiding you?"

"Aunt Lucy's spirit? How ridiculous! I told you I don't believe in that nonsense!"

"What's wrong, Araby?" Daul's voice was tinged with amusement, but his facial expression was hidden in the darkness. "Aren't you comfortable talking about Aunt Lucy's spirit?"

"I don't believe such a thing exists," she persisted stubbornly. Actually the subject did make her uneasy.

"I don't know, Araby. I feel very comfortable here with Aunt Lucy. I kinda like it."

"Daul, that's crazy! I think I'll turn in for the night. I can see the conversation is sliding into nonsense." Araby stood and fumbled her way to the door, thinking they should have left a light on somewhere.

"Araby . . ." Daul's hand rested on her arm, restraining her gently. "Don't go . . ."

"Daul . . ." Her voice trailed off as his lips met hers, sweet and persuasive.

There was no resisting as Araby found herself sinking into his arms. Their embrace was as natural and easy as the entire evening had been. His lips claimed hers in an affirmation of desire, his tongue tingling her sensitive mouth, tempting the inevitable.

Araby leaned against Daul, grateful for the strength he exuded, the support he offered. His chest was expansive and hard and her hand crept up, touching the dark curls above the top button of his plaid shirt.

"Daul, no," she breathed as he moved his seducing lips from hers down the creamy column of her arched neck.

"Araby, don't you see how naturally we fit together? This entire evening has been so comfortable. So easy. We belong together. All night long . . ."

She took a deep breath. "No, Daul. We don't belong together. We're not alike at all. We can't give in to one moment of p-passion." She pushed at his shoulders with weak hands.

"What about the glory of a night of passion? You want me, Araby. Admit it. I can feel it too."

"I . . . I can't. This has been a special evening, Daul. One I'll remember for a long time. Thank you. But I have to go—" She heaved herself away from his warmth and escaped to the darkness of her bedroom, hating herself more every minute.

Oh, dear God, she wanted him. Desperately. Wanted to let him make love to her. She felt shaky and on fire for the first time in her life. Oh, she'd been kissed before, but no kisses lifted her off the floor like Daul's. Still, she wouldn't give in to her lust. After all, he wasn't her type. There was no future for them together.

She began to undress in the darkness, and when her eyes became adjusted to the dimness she could see the cherry-wood heart on the dresser. Its solid smoothness invited her touch and she caressed it before opening the lid. Before the music could begin playing Araby snapped the lid shut, telling herself it would be all wrong. She'd be gone in two days. Then what? She had another life in Nashville. And it did not include Daul McNeal.

Eventually, Araby fell into a fitful sleep. It was sometime after midnight when she was awakened by the clearly recognizable voice of her dear, departed Aunt Lucy!

CHAPTER FIVE

In the attic . . .

Alarmed, Araby bolted upright in bed. "What? Who's there?" Someone was speaking to her, nearby, in the same room! And the voice was definitely female!

Then she heard the voice again. . . . *chest in the attic* . . . The words were clear and sounded as much like Aunt Lucy as Araby could remember.

She strained to detect a figure in the darkness. Was that a shadow in the window? "W-Who's there?" she repeated, listening intently. The sheer lace curtain billowed in a faint breeze. But there was no other sound.

Then who woke her? Could it possibly be Daul, slipping into her room? Oh, he wouldn't dare! Instinctively, Araby pulled the green and gold lily quilt to her breast. And listened. But no, it couldn't be Daul. It had been a woman's voice. She was sure of it.

There was no sound other than the wild pounding of her heart. There were no human shadows, nothing moving, just a whiff of a breeze ruffling the lace curtain. And yet Araby was positive she had heard someone. But who? She reached back into her subconscious, trying to recapture a distant dream she couldn't quite remember.

She pressed her hands to her forehead, trying to force the dream to the surface. But it wasn't like a dream. It was like . . . the real thing. She had heard Aunt Lucy as clear as a bell. Something about the chest in the attic. Her eyes widened as an image flickered, then disappeared.

"Oh, my God! It couldn't be Aunt Lucy!"

Suddenly, Araby was frightened. In one long-legged leap she was out of bed, calling for the only one who could understand this. "Daul! Daul! Help me! Oh, Daul!" She no longer feared that someone was in the room. She was convinced it was Aunt Lucy's spirit.

Blindly she ran, bolting through the house, calling frantically. She climbed the steep stairs to the attic. The next thing she knew she was in Daul's arms, his hands caressing her shoulders, his bare chest giving her solid comfort.

His voice rumbled through her, erasing her fear. "Easy now, sweetheart. It's all right. Everything's fine. What happened? Did you have a bad dream?"

"Oh no! It . . . it wasn't a dream!" Araby clung frantically to him with her eyes squeezed shut. "It was . . . Aunt . . . Lucy." She finished brokenly, finally realizing how inane she sounded. "Oh, Daul, that sounds so dumb. I . . . I guess I was dreaming, after all."

"Araby . . . sweetheart, don't be scared. I'm here with you. And we're alone." His words sounded so reassuring.

"She was right there. I heard her!"

"It's just you and me, Araby."

"I could see her shadow in the lace curtain. Wispy and vague. She told me . . ."

Daul's hand stroked her shoulder. "She's been on your mind all day."

Araby opened her eyes. "She said . . . 'the chest in the attic' as plain as day. I . . . I swear it, Daul!" Her words still came in spurts as she tried to catch her breath and clear her mind at the same time.

"All right, sweetheart. Whatever you say." He pulled her close, his body giving her more comfort than mere words ever could. Together they sank to a sitting position on the top stair, neither cognizant of how long they stayed there, arms entwined.

"Daul, what's wrong with me?" Araby's voice was small in the darkness. "Am I losing my mind?"

"Noooo. College professors don't lose their minds."

"They just believe in ghosts?"

"You're experiencing some unexplained phenomenon during a particularly stressful time."

"You sound like a shrink." She muffled the words as she turned her face against his bare chest, her lips burrowing in the crisp curls. "I must be going crazy."

"No, you aren't. You're perfectly normal, Araby.

This old farmhouse just brings out lots of old memories. You loved dear old Aunt Lucy, and it isn't easy to forget about her."

She sighed. "Yes, that's it. Packing her things away has been one of the hardest things I've ever done. She's rebelling at being relegated to a photo album." Araby gasped at her own words. "Oh God, I sound like she's right here. I *am* losing my mind!"

Daul's voice softened. "Maybe she *is* here. Who knows?"

"Good grief, Daul! You don't actually believe that!"

"I don't know what to believe. Maybe her spirit's still drifting around." He said it lightly, but neither of them laughed.

Araby loosened her bear hold around his chest and looked at him strangely. "Now I think you've lost your marbles!"

"We're in this together, Araby. Me and you and . . . Aunt Lucy." His crooked finger stroked her cheek. "But it's okay. I told you before, I feel at ease with her around here. We belong together. You and me."

"And Aunt Lucy?"

"Hmmm, maybe."

"You aren't laughing at me, are you, Daul?"

"Of course not, sweetheart. I care too much about you to laugh." His stroking finger trailed down to her chin and tilted it upward. With a great deal of tenderness he kissed her lips.

She sighed and gave in to the fullness of another

kiss, feeling as she had never felt with any other man. The kiss ignited spirals of pleasure she had never imagined possible. Her head rolled back, her lips opening slightly to accommodate the perfect match of his lips.

When his finger was no longer needed to lift her chin, he allowed it to trail sensuously down the curve of her neck and dip into the heated crevasse between her breasts.

"Araby, sweetheart, you're a wonder. I have never felt so right with any woman. You're perfect for me." His kisses lit trails of fire over her flushed cheeks and down the hot flesh of her neck to the gentle swell of her breasts. His hand slipped inside the wispy lace nightgown and cupped one breast, appreciating its fullness, its automatic response to his touch.

"Araby, I want to see you. I want you. All of you."

"Yes, Daul," she murmured between kisses. "I've never felt this way before, not this . . . strongly."

He kissed her again as his hands deftly eased the gown straps over her shoulders and let the lacy bodice drop to her waist. "Ah, beautiful!" He bent to caress her breasts with velvety lips, laving each nipple with his tongue.

She moaned softly and leaned into his glorious kisses. "Daul, I'm weak." She felt the flush of desire course through her body.

"They are just as I imagined, as I dreamed they would be. Oh yes, I've dreamed of touching you,

Araby. Like this . . . and this. They are so soft and . . . touchable." He kissed her breasts lavishly, then lifted his lips to hers while his fingertips continued to set her afire.

His hands covered each of the twin, creamy mounds, his palms gently massaging them. Unable to move away from his caresses, Araby looked into the smoky gray depths of his passion-darkened eyes. "Only you make me feel this way, Daul." She was consumed with wildfire. With every word, every fiery moment, she wanted him more.

"That's because we belong together, Araby. You and me. We're all that matter in the entire world tonight." His hands continued their maddening magic on her flesh.

With every breathless word, every heated touch, she wanted him more. In fact, she had never wanted a man to make love to her more in her life.

Love? Was she really thinking of love? Or did Daul just know how to ignite those sparks of desire deep inside her? Araby tossed aside her doubts, her reasoning. She only knew that she wanted to lie in his arms tonight. Wanted to pull him to her warmth. Maybe he was right. They did belong together, at least for now.

Araby lifted her hands to the masculine expanse of his bare chest, her fingers moving slowly across the breadth of his shoulders. With wanton pleasure she pressed her pliable breasts to his muscular chest, relishing the tickling of his crispy chest hairs on her aroused and sensitive skin.

His strong hands spread across her back, caressing until she shuddered against him. Then he stood, pulling her to her feet with him. His widespread legs braced on either side of her thighs as he encompassed her body with his.

"Make love to me, Daul," she whispered. She could feel his arousal with only her thin, filmy gown between them.

"Araby, are you sure?"

"Yes! We belong together!" She urged him with sensuous, undulating body motions. "You said it yourself, and it's true."

"I want you . . . Araby. All of you. . . ." After he pulled the white gown down over her hips and let it drop to a limp circle at her feet, he took off his cutoff jeans. They stood, hot and passion-filled, but not touching, for a long moment. He breathed deeply, raggedly, as his eyes traveled over her, ravaging her . . . caressing her. "Oh God . . ." he murmured.

"Daul, touch me," she whispered, aching for his complete fulfillment.

Pulling on all his male reserve, Daul used feather-soft strokes, his callused, musician's fingertips starting at the swell of her breasts, brushing downward. He twirled the taut, darkened tips, then reached her waist, encircling it with both hands. He stroked her hips, allowing his fingers to trail around her thighs to the sensitive inner flesh. Gently, he pressed the center of her desire. His probing generated a slow, methodical rotation of her hips, and her breathing came in short spurts.

As she thrust against him with growing intensity they sank together onto the antique iron bedstead.

"Araby, touch me . . . here . . . ah, sweet . . ."

"Kiss me again, Daul. Love me . . ."

"Easy . . ."

"Don't wait, Daul. Hurry!"

Muffled words and expressions of pleasure gave way to a frenzied passion as both rose in the swirl of ecstasy. It was ancient and exotic and completely satisfying, a rapturous splendor, a heightening of senses, a lifting of two together in glory.

In a stretch of joy they reached the ultimate of pleasure's peak. Reality meandered slowly into a relaxed comfort as they lay entwined, drifting in slumber. They were half awake, half asleep, resplendent and sated. It was a special feeling, a wonderful sharing, an acceptance that what was happening between them was all that mattered in the world.

"I take it back," Daul mumbled into her blond hair.

"Huh?"

"What I said about you not knowing about a climax."

"Thanks to you, I have no excuses." She smiled and nestled against his chest. "But that doesn't mean I don't have more to learn."

"Is that a hint?"

"Ummm. What do you think?" She kissed his chest and rested her head there so she could listen to the beat of his heart.

Later they awoke again to partake of sexual pleasures, to learn about each other, to enjoy each other to the fullest, to give complete and fulfilling satisfaction. This time the loving was slower, more intense, yet more satisfying. When they had finished satisfying each other they slept for the remainder of the night with their arms around each other.

The next morning Araby woke early and slipped out of bed, leaving Daul sleeping with his proud, dark head thrown back and the blue and white quilt rumpled at his waist. She smiled contentedly as she gazed at him for a long, yearning moment. His gentle caring last night had turned to passion, a passion the likes of which Araby had never known or experienced. Was that all it was for them? Passion?

She pressed her hand to her heart, struck with another thought. Was this what Daul meant when he said, "Aunt Lucy and I have a deal. I'll get you yet"?

Perturbed, Araby grabbed her gown and descended from their attic love nest. What did he mean by his bold claim? Could it be true? Who was this strange man who seemed to communicate with spirits? This man who took her to bed and turned her into a wanton, sensual being? All she knew was that, because of Aunt Lucy, she had spent the night in his arms!

She slipped the gown on and started the coffee, her mind racing with thoughts of Daul McNeal and their passionate night together. Whatever had come over her, to be so free with her body? She had never been so . . . so shamelessly erotic. Nor had she ever felt such a high degree of passion for any man.

Last night she had wanted him savagely. Perhaps she had been the seducer! Yes! In fact she had seduced him by going upstairs! It was almost as if . . . he had cast a spell on her, turning her into the seductress. Well, that cinched it! She had to finish her work here and get away from this farm. Away from Daul's spell and . . . Aunt Lucy's influence. Araby poured herself a cup of coffee and didn't notice the gentle gray eyes observing her.

Daul paused in the doorway, surveying Araby's image in the misty morning light as she stood at the window sipping coffee. She had slipped so willingly into his arms, made love so passionately during the night, he wasn't sure it was the same fancy lady with the spicy tongue he'd been sparring with all week. He couldn't understand the swell of emotion that engulfed him as he stood there, impelling him to take her in his arms, to care for her.

"Coffee smells good," he commented, entering the room. "Mind if I join you?"

Araby turned around to face him, and all her doubts flew away. The spell was cast, and she smiled. There was no resentment, no anger in her expression. Only contentment, satisfaction, a calm composure. "Sure. Help yourself. But don't think I'm going to do this every morning."

He poured himself a cup of the strong brew and

103

met her eyes with a gray twinkle. "Don't think I can do that every night."

She grinned at his insinuation. "How disappointing. I thought you had so much more to teach me."

"I do. But I'm only human. And aging fast." His long-fingered hand stroked the beard where dashes of gray were clearly visible now among the black strands. Each day brought the beard to a richer, thicker luster and Araby was beginning to like it. Very much.

"College professors are human too. And capable of enjoying an occasional climax."

"So I noticed. I'm glad to see you don't regret what happened."

She shrugged. "How could I? I'm a consenting adult. Last night it appeared that I was the seducer."

"And I was more than eager to be seduced by you. Araby, I—"

She lifted her palm to restrain him. "Please, don't say anything, Daul. No statements you'll regret later."

"I can assure you that I don't regret a moment of last night." His gray eyes were honest.

"Tell me something, Daul." She refilled her coffee cup and turned a serious face to him. "Is that what you meant when you said you and Aunt Lucy have a deal? You knew I'd come to you?"

He shrugged. "Something like that."

"Are you saying she's spoken to you?" Araby

sidled closer, her blue eyes narrowing slightly as she looked at him.

"No. That privilege is reserved for you."

"Then . . . what? How?"

"I don't know how to explain it, Araby. All I have is a feeling. And it's a strong one. If anything, I just feel in harmony with this house. Even with the notion of Aunt Lucy's spirit floating around here. Does that make any sense?"

She arched her eyebrows. "After last night I don't know what makes sense. Maybe she's got us both under her spell."

"Maybe. But if last night is an example, it isn't a bad spell to be under, is it?"

"No, I guess not. . . ."

He set both their coffee cups on the counter and draped his arms over her shoulders. "Kiss me, Araby. Prove that I wasn't dreaming about last night."

She moved closer to him, snuggling contentedly against his lean frame. "It was a wonderful dream." She inhaled his clean, masculine scent and gave in to a longer kiss.

"Araby . . . my sweet Araby . . ." His hands roamed over her back, molding her entirely to his hard length.

"Daul . . ." Once again there was no resisting him, no holding back. Mesmerized, she gave in to the sweep of emotions that flooded her when she was in his arms.

The kiss deepened as his tongue plunged past hers to the honeyed recesses of her mouth. Then in one sweeping motion he lifted her into his arms and carried her into the bedroom next to the kitchen. "Let's see if Aunt Lucy's bed is any softer than the one in the attic."

"That mattress is specially made," Araby giggled as they tumbled together onto the green and gold quilt. "But since heat rises, it's cooler down here than in the attic."

"Specially made for us," he murmured as kisses rained over her face and neck. "Let's see if we can warm this place up a bit."

"Daul!" She glowed with a growing desire as he stripped off her lacy gown again.

He stood to divest himself of the cutoff jeans, and Araby stretched and preened like a cat. A luxurious kitten, sprawled on a rumpled green and gold North Carolina lily quilt. Her silken hair fanned around her head, and she rested both arms on either side.

When Daul could endure watching her erotic motions no longer, he wrapped himself in her welcoming arms. They twisted in ecstasy as he thrust firmly into the feminine warmth she offered. He found her petal-soft and eager, her desire high. She pressed her silky-smooth skin to his, the contrast of their textures arousing him to distraction.

Together they swirled in rapture's glory . . . round and round . . . again and again . . . quickly reaching the climax they sought . . . slowly returning to earth . . . to the present.

Later they bathed each other with warm bubbles in the old-fashioned, claw-footed bathtub.

"Ah, this is wonderful, Araby! They don't make tubs like this any more." Daul hunched with his broad back as she scrubbed energetically.

Araby's legs straddled his hips as she raked over every inch of his back with a soapy cloth. "Enough of this! Now it's my turn!"

He rotated to face her, both hands scaling up the length of her thighs. "My pleasure!"

In the midst of the most glorious bath she'd ever had, Araby paused long enough to allow noises from the outside world to enter. "Listen, Daul." She sat upright, sloshing water on the floor with her sudden motion. "I hear a truck. It must be Mr. Calhoun here to get the hay."

Daul didn't even try to hide his disappointment. "They start early here in the country, don't they?"

"Not as early as you do!" She tweaked his nose. "Come on! We can't lie around all day. We have work to do!"

"Aw, and I wanted to lie around all day! With you!" He watched her step out of the tub and moaned, "We haven't even had breakfast yet."

"Don't you ever think of anything except your stomach?" She flicked the towel over her backside.

"As a matter of fact I was thinking of something else just now!" He unplugged the tub, heaved himself out, and grabbed the towel she threw his way. "But it has nothing to do with loading hay. Maybe rolling in it!"

She disappeared into the bedroom. "Hurry, Daul!"

"Now where have I heard that before?"

Just as he finished drying his back a wrinkled pair of cutoff jeans hit him squarely on the head.

They sat on the front porch watching lightning bugs dance in the darkness.

"How do you feel?"

"Mixed. Sort of good. Somewhat sad."

"Aunt Lucy would approve of what you did to-day."

"I know."

"Calhoun even found someone to buy the tractor. And the flatbed trailer."

"Yeah."

"You don't sound very enthusiastic. And the preacher knew several families who could use the furniture."

"Wait'll they see all those knickknacks!" Araby forced a little chuckle.

"They'll probably be delighted. Anyway, you couldn't keep everything, Araby."

"I know. But it looks so bare in there."

They nestled together in the porch swing, contented with each other's presence.

"That's the way a house looks when you clear it out." His arm slid around her shoulders, squeezing her reassuringly to him.

"I don't know why, but I saved the beds. And a couple of antique tables. And, of course, the piano."

"They appear to be genuine antiques. I'm sure they're valuable."

"But I don't have room for them in my Nashville apartment."

"They belong on the farm. Leave them here. We'll put them to good use."

She laid her head on his shoulder and smiled, grateful that Daul was with her right now. She needed him, needed his assurances, needed his funny quips. She did not want to be alone tonight.

After a moment of silence he commented dryly, "Actually, I like the old iron bedstead in the attic best."

"Me too."

"Let's go try it out again."

"Okay."

"Your lack of enthusiasm discourages me."

"Sorry. Can I help it if it's been a bummer of a day?"

"Don't tell me you aren't in the mood," he drawled.

"Okay. I won't say it."

"Well, are you in the mood for a little gift from Aunt Lucy?"

"I'm not in the mood to make light of the situation. I feel bad enough as it is."

"I'm serious. Today I found something very special that once belonged to her. And I think she wanted to share it with us."

Araby raised her head to look at his dark image. "What are you talking about?"

"Love letters. I found a whole bunch, tied together, stuffed in the bottom drawer of that chest in the attic before the preacher and I moved it."

"The chest in the attic?" she repeated slowly, her words coming in soft whispers, her heart pounding. "That's what Aunt Lucy said—"

"Yep. So, you see, she wanted us to find them before you gave away the chest."

Araby's eyes grew large. "Oh my God, Daul . . ."

CHAPTER SIX

Araby leaned against the kitchen table and absently watched Daul. "Do you really think we should read them?"

"Of course. But we have to be in the right mood." Daul filled the bottom of the pan with corn oil and set it on the stove. With meticulous care he dropped three corn kernels into the oil and clapped the lid on, tight.

"I don't know, Daul. Smacks of invading privacy to me."

"Why, Araby, you've been invading Aunt Lucy's privacy all week! What do you call going through all her stuff? Anyway, I'm convinced she wanted us to read these letters." When the three kernels exploded, Daul poured enough golden kernels into the pan to cover the bottom and watched as they began to sizzle. Covering them, he smiled with satisfaction. "They'll be ready in a minute."

"Why do you think she wanted us to read them?" she asked.

He turned around and pinched her nose affectionately. "That's what we'll find out when we read them!"

She shook her head. "I should have known you'd say that. Circular reasoning."

Multiple tiny explosions caused him to turn his complete attention to the pan on the stove, and he began a lengthy dissertation on the theory of popcorn-making. "Now here comes the very best popcorn, prepared the old-fashioned way by the popcorn king of Nashville! There were no air poppers or microwave ovens in the good ole days. And I'll bet Aunt Lucy knew this secret to getting all those stubborn little kernels to pop."

"I always wondered . . ." she observed dryly.

He shook the pan over the heat a couple of times, then rubbed his hands together in anticipation. "You make sure the temperature of the oil is sufficient by giving it a few test kernels. When they pop, it's hot enough. Then when you add the rest, preferably straight from the freezer, they have no alternative but to pop."

"No alternative, huh?" she quipped wryly. "And that, kiddies, is the popcorn king's cooking lesson for the day."

"Scoff if you will. But Orville Redenbacher took popcorn lessons from me! Would you get the wine, please?" He motioned toward the refrigerator. "This'll be ready in a jiffy."

"Wine? With popcorn?" Araby made a face behind his back but extracted the chilled wine as he directed.

"Of course! It's fabulous! Weren't you ever a college student on a budget? Cheap red wine and popcorn makes seventeenth-century European history much more palatable." Once the popping stopped, Daul moved quickly to dump the popcorn into a huge crockery bowl, one that Aunt Lucy had undoubtedly used for the same ingredients. "Plus, I figure it'll set the mood for reading old love letters. Or making love. Or, if neither of those work, maybe we can write a song."

"Ah-ha! You just want me to do your work for you!" Araby opened the nearly empty cabinet and grasped the two crystal goblets they had used for wine the previous night.

"Not a bad idea." He sprinkled Parmesan cheese over the old-fashioned popcorn and shook it around a little. "Much better for you than salt and butter. Ready?"

"I have my part." Araby lifted the chilled wine and goblets. "Now all we need is a good old Tennessee toad strangler, known in other parts as a heavy rainstorm," she laughed as they clattered upstairs together, spilling popcorn as they tried to feed each other. "One that lasts all night, and you just love to curl up and listen to the rain on the roof."

"If you sit very still and quiet for a few minutes," Daul informed her, "you'll hear the mice playing in the roof space, and you can pretend it's rain."

"Mice! I thought your calico mouser caught them all."

"Oh, she cleared out the majority. Kept them from running over my feet at night. But there're

113

plenty more. Anyway, Mama-cat has slowed down considerably. She's probably due to become a mother any day now."

Araby inspected the corners of the semivacant attic. "Well, where is she?"

He shrugged. "I haven't seen her in a few days. She's probably making a nest somewhere. Maybe in the barn."

"Then she's not nesting up here? I'm surprised. Did you see her today when you were helping Mr. Calhoun load the hay?"

"No, but I didn't spend much time looking for the cat. Actually, I don't think she feels safe enough to have her babies in here. She isn't very trusting of people. . . . Why? Are you suddenly concerned about the orphan cat?"

"No." Araby sniffed indifferently. "But the way you took her in and defended her, one would think she'd be eternally grateful and stick with you through thick and thin."

"Cats are fickle." Daul heaved himself on the turkey tracks quilt, settled the bowl in his lap, and began to toss the popcorn in the air and catch it in his mouth.

"Play me a love song, Daul," Araby encouraged gently.

"What's wrong? Don't you want to play my game? Open up. I'll bet I can hit the bull's-eye." He closed one eye and pretended to take aim at her mouth.

She shook her head with a smile and scooted in beside him. "Come on. Play something."

"You sure?" He glanced at her doubtfully. "We're talking simple acoustic guitar accompaniment here, not a twenty-piece orchestra."

"You play," she directed. "I'll pour. Unless you'd rather sit here all night speculating on Mama-cat's condition and tossing popcorn in the air."

"Oh no. I'd rather get on to the mood-setting." He replaced the popcorn bowl in his lap with the well-worn sandalwood guitar and sang a short ditty asking the crucial question "Does Your Chewing Gum Lose Its Flavor on the Bedpost Overnight?"

"That's to put me in the mood for love?" she laughed and handed him a goblet of wine.

"No, that's to lift your spirits. Er . . . no pun intended, Aunt Lucy!" He raised his glass high. "Here's to . . . Aunt Lucy's love letters."

Araby sipped, then held her glass up for another toast. "And to the award-winning sound track by the fabulous Daul McNeal! You *are* writing a sound track, aren't you?"

He plunked a C chord. "Here-here!"

"Please, play something good and . . . romantic," she directed and grabbed a handful of popcorn.

"What would you like to hear? Something schmaltzy?"

"Yeah." She grinned. "Actually, I'd like to hear the collective masterpieces you created in the middle of the night when you kept me awake! I want to know what you did all those miserable hours while I had to listen to those same chords over and over." She rolled onto her back and balanced the wineglass on her flat belly.

"What I did, mostly, was keep the cat awake."

"And me," she added.

"And you." He agreed. "Actually, I couldn't get you out of my mind. What I should do is write a love song about a beautiful, spicy, blond lady with daring blue eyes who likes to eat quiche and watch lightning bugs."

Araby's blue eyes twinkled merrily, and she turned on her side. "No, no, no! That'll never make it. Don't you know what makes a country song successful?"

He looked down his nose at her. "If I knew the answer to that million-dollar question, I wouldn't be sitting here in your attic. Tree would be paying me full-time and I'd send them top-of-the-chart winners from some exotic island!"

"Tree?"

"Tree International. A music-publishing company in Nashville."

"Well, we won't tell them the secret. Actually, it shouldn't be too hard to figure out." She clucked her tongue teasingly.

"It isn't blue-eyed blondes who drop popcorn all over my bed? And keep trying to spill the wine?"

She giggled and refilled their glasses. "That's far too schmaltzy. Here are the crucial ingredients. You have to mention mama, and trains, and drinkin', and prison, and rain, and, let's see . . . oh yes, pickup trucks!"

"Damn, Araby!" Daul hooted with laughter.

116

"For a fancy lady who snobbishly pretends not to care about country music, you seem to know a helluva lot about it! You've listened to a few country songs along the way!"

"Oh, maybe a couple," she conceded with a grin. "Now, play something for me. I want to hear your newest creation."

"Ah, my blue-eyed Fancy Lady, you're full of surprises." He leaned forward and kissed her lips. "How about collaborating on a song about listening to rain on the roof while drinkin' cheap wine and eatin' popcorn with a sexy blond professor in the attic where she made me her prisoner after I gave her a ride from the train station in my pickup truck?" He paused and inhaled dramatically.

She laughed. "You left out mama."

"With Mama-cat in the corner, the best calico mouser in Tennessee . . ." he added.

"I think you've got it."

"I only want you, sexy blond lady. . . ."

She moved her lips sensuously against his. "The mood isn't set yet. You haven't even gotten to the love songs."

"Hard-drivin' woman," he grumbled and played a couple of partially completed songs, then stopped in disgust. "Awful! I'm depressing myself! What I need is a good, juicy love letter." He reached for the dusty stack of envelopes bound together with a faded blue ribbon.

"How do you know they're love letters? Maybe they're from Aunt Lucy's sister back East."

"I just have a feeling." He began to sort through them. "How about somebody from Atlanta?"

Araby raised her eyebrows. "Must have been when Uncle John went to Atlanta to work one winter. Daul? Are you sure we want to do this?"

"Positive! Let's see now. This seems to be the earliest postmark. We want to get this story from the very beginning."

"Story? Do you really think there's a story here?"

"Why else would she have saved them? And encouraged us to read them?"

"I can't answer to the last part, but the first is because she was a hopeless romantic." Araby shrugged.

Daul opened the wafer-thin, ecru paper and read aloud, " 'My Dearest Lucy, Hearing from you again was a joy. But seeing you was a ray of sunshine in my otherwise drab life. You have brought laughter to my heart again. I'll never forget our weekend together. . . .' "

"Oh, how sweet, Daul," Araby cooed softly. "Uncle John missed her so much, he was inspired to write this poetic little letter to tell her how much he enjoyed her visit. People don't write letters like that anymore. They send a Hallmark card that says everything for them."

"Only when they want to send the very best," he reminded her with a tight smile.

"Nothing could be better than a personal statement from the heart."

"Well, this one was with love from Jake." Daul finished reading and started to fold the letter.

"John," she corrected. "It was Uncle John."

Daul looked closely at the signature. "This says 'Love, Jake.'"

"Couldn't be. Let me see that." Araby sat up quickly and sloshed her rosy wine on the quilt in the process. "Oh, damn!"

His long arm engulfed her shoulders, and he nuzzled her earlobe. "Don't worry about it. You can spill wine in my bed anytime, sweetheart. Hey, that sounds like a line from a song!"

"I think that one's been taken, or at least something close. No, it was crackers in bed. Are you going to let me see that signature?" She reached for the letter and scrutinized it for herself. "Daul, you're right! It says Jake. Who the hell is Jake? Let's take a look at another one."

"What happened to the person who didn't want to invade Aunt Lucy's privacy?"

"That person has changed her mind. This could be serious if these letters aren't from Uncle John." Araby hurriedly opened another envelope. "It isn't! This one says 'Jake' too! 'Love, Jake'!"

"Ah-ha! I knew there was a story here!" Daul exclaimed with satisfaction. "Read on!"

Araby cleared her throat. "'My Darling Lucy, I've decided to accept the offer to visit you in Tennessee. I'll be there next week. Anxiously waiting to hold you in my arms again. Love, Jake.'" Araby looked up excitedly. "Daul, I'll bet this is the man who came to stay with Aunt Lucy that

119

summer! I knew he wasn't here to fix the barn roof! Do you realize what we've discovered here?"

"Ain't it obvious?" He winked and held his empty wineglass out for another refill.

Araby poured more wine into both goblets and sat Indian style in the middle of the bed. "Read the next one, Daul!"

For the next full hour the story of Aunt Lucy's love affair with an old boyfriend began to emerge. After Uncle John's death Aunt Lucy contacted a man named Jake in Atlanta. They exchanged visits, and letters, and their love flowered anew. But their differences were great.

"I'll read awhile." Araby nestled her head comfortably in Daul's lap and picked up one of the few remaining letters. " 'My Darling Sweetheart, My heart is heavy as I write this. I'm afraid our new love could never surpass our differences.'

" 'I do not consider smoking ladylike, and I could never abide your aggravating habit of taking in strays, like that pregnant girl you befriended. The biggest obstacle is the social stigma of marrying a cousin, however distant our kinship may be. I know you said that our love is all that matters, but my darling Lucy, I don't think things would work out. . . .' " Araby halted her reading, struggling to retain her composure. "Oh, Daul, how sad. This is a 'good-bye' letter."

He took the letter. "There's more. Want me to read it? 'P.S. Please keep the music box as a token of my love. You will always be my sweetheart. . . .' "

120

Araby's eyes welled with tears. "The cherry-wood heart is a gift from Jake. So that's why it was hidden. How sweet . . . and sad."

"A bit schmaltzy, I'd say," Daul said, laying the letter aside. His hand moved to her waist.

"I guess," Araby conceded softly. "This is a side of Aunt Lucy I never considered. Loving and losing."

"Makes her seem very human to me." His hand ventured beneath her blouse. "Loving and losing is a part of real life. It's what I know best, what I write about. I think she wanted us to know this story."

"Do you?" She smiled lazily as his hand moved up to cup one of her breasts and a warmth began to spread through her. His touch acted as an aphrodisiac, and her appetite for more of his spellbinding touches increased rapidly.

Daul shifted closer. "Araby, we—you and I—have something special here. And I don't want to lose it." His lips met hers, gently at first, nibbling and teasing. When she quivered with eager response, his kiss became deeper, a fervent claim on her lips, an ardent promise to possess her body.

"You're special to me, Daul. I'm so lucky to have tumbled down those stairs into your arms."

"Oh God, sweetheart, I don't want to lose you. Not yet."

The thought of leaving hadn't crossed her mind all day. However, it was inevitable, eventually. Daul's lament reminded Araby that she couldn't bear the thought of leaving, either. She only wanted to lie in his strong arms, to feel his kisses all over her body, to know again the fulfillment of his love. To make love throughout the night.

"Hold me, Daul," she murmured, raising her arms to encircle his broad shoulders. "Never let me go."

His kisses fluttered like spring butterflies over her face, from her closed eyelids to her partly opened lips. She arched her neck so those butterflies could trail downward to caress her bare breasts. Hot kisses lit tiny fires around the pale, heaving mounds, inflaming her deepest feminine urges. The taut tips of her breasts yearned for him even before his lips closed firmly over them. He tugged on the surging nipples until they were crimson, swollen, and eager.

"Oh God, Araby . . . you're so beautiful! And all mine!"

"So what . . . are you . . . waiting for?" she teased, knowing the sight of her aroused flesh tempted him, knowing she could hardly wait for his fulfillment.

"You, Fancy Lady . . ."

Her fingers dove for the snap on his jeans and within minutes both of them lay nude and wanting on the narrow attic bed with its blue turkey tracks. But Araby wasn't content to wait for his obvious pleasure. Her smooth hands raked over his masculine planes stroking and admiring. She excited and enlivened every sensitive area of his body, triggering an inner frenzy of passion as her fingertips tantalized his skin, her lips added liquid fire to the expanding volcano within him.

While her fingers massaged his arms and shoulders her kisses covered his chest, testing the hardness of his nipples, burying deeply in the mat of crisp hair that spread gloriously across the muscular expanse. Her curious tongue followed the trail of dark hair down his flat belly to dip into his navel, then proceeded lower.

Using skills she never knew she had and techniques she had never employed, Araby brought him to a dizzying height of desire.

Daul's low groan accompanied the shudder that racked his body as he gathered her to him. "Araby —your fingers are magic. But your body drives me crazy. I need you now!"

"How's this?" She settled her warm femininity over him, then gyrated slowly, maddeningly. Moving with erotic purpose, she brought them both to the brink, then paused.

"Araby . . ." His hands guided her hips.

"Do you like it?"

His response was more of a guttural rasp than a word. "Don't stop moving. . . ."

She moved with him as their desire grew more urgent and reckless.

Together in glory they swirled, two heated bodies attaining the ultimate in unison. His cry of her name echoed again and again with each thrust.

"Araby . . . Araby . . . Araby . . . Araby!"

Suddenly time stood still and emotions reached to the depths of their souls, each lost in a passionate frenzy. There were no more words, no thoughts, nothing in the world mattered except their love.

In the misty quiet that followed, two bodies were wrapped together as if to preserve the heated furor they had created. But the peaks slowly melted into a warm flow of feelings, a silent knowledge that what they shared was indeed special, something close to a love that neither would admit. They would acknowledge only a fulfillment of their lusty appetites, a satisfaction of sexual urges. For now that's what they clung to, for neither had ever felt such deep pleasure.

"You're full of surprises, sweetheart." He shifted beneath her. "You are quite a temptress."

"You're good inspiration." Araby kissed him and with her fingers traced patterns in the damp curls on his chest. "Listen. I think I hear rain."

His hand followed the feminine curve of her back and hips. "Me too. It's so nice to lie here and listen to it hitting the roof. To lie here with you. . . ."

A sudden whiff of wind billowed the lacy curtains, cooling the warm attic air. The two lovers stirred, but continued to cling together, holding fast to each other and love . . . throughout the night.

Araby stayed at the old farmhouse longer than she had planned. She and Daul found the September days weren't long enough for their shared joys, the nights too short for their insatiable passions.

They switched roles and Daul became the teacher; Araby, the eager student. He relished the teaching. She delighted in the learning.

They hiked the rolling hills around the farm, walked through a scented pine forest, picnicked beside a meandering stream, climbed huge granite and marble boulders, frolicked in the icy spray of a waterfall. The heat of summer flew, leaving the nip of autumn in one short week. A cold gray drizzle was falling the morning she decided to leave.

"You know I have to go, Daul. School starts soon and, unless I want to lose my job, I have to report."

"You wouldn't consider losing your job?" He stuffed his hands into the pockets of his jeans, drawing the material tight over his thighs.

She flushed with warmth, remembering the way those muscular thighs felt alongside hers. Hard and sturdy and forceful. "It's difficult to pay the rent without a job." She turned back to her suitcase and neatly packed the last of her clothes.

"Tonight is going to be damn cold in that attic without you."

"Why don't you take the downstairs bedroom by the kitchen where it's warmer?" She smiled wanly. "We'll be together in Nashville soon. We both have work to do. You have a sound track to write, remember?"

"Vaguely." He ran a hand over his face. "At least I'm full of the needed emotions. Especially the 'lost-my-woman blues.'"

"Daul, I'm not leaving you completely. I'll see you in Nashville. We'll be together then."

His voice was empty. "It'll be different there."

"No, it won't. It'll be better." She picked up the cherry-wood heart and started to stuff it in the suitcase.

His large hands covered hers. Together they lifted the lid. *Let me hear you whisper . . .*

Their eyes met in a pledge of love, their lips melded in an unavoidable declaration. As they embraced, the music box tumbled on the bed. *. . . that you love me too . . .*

"Daul. I have to go," she reminded him gently.

"Then, go!" Abruptly, he pushed her away.

"I hate this too."

"Then, go quickly. Don't prolong it."

"Maybe I should have slipped away in the night, so I wouldn't disturb you! I have feelings, too, you know!"

His gray eyes softened. "Sorry. I'm making this harder for both of us."

"Let me make it easier." She dug into the top drawer of the antique chest in the corner. "Here. This is for you." She thrust a large manila envelope into his hands.

"What—"

"My poems. They're for you. Use them if you want to. If not . . ." She shrugged as if it didn't matter. But they both knew it did.

"You didn't mail them off?"

"Nope. I figured I was stupid to pass up the opportunity to have them published in a song, es-

126

pecially since I know a real, live songwriter so intimately."

"Even if I put them in a country-music song? Are you sure, Araby? We're talking about guitars and fiddles. Smoky barrooms. 'Lost-my-woman blues.'"

She nodded. "I'm sure. In fact, I'd be honored . . ."

His arms wrapped around her and their secure warmth and the taste of his kiss lingered with her long after she'd left Aunt Lucy's old farm.

Daul watched her drive away in the slow rain. "Araby, sweetheart, you're full of surprises." He climbed the stairs to the attic, flung himself on the turkey tracks quilt, and stared for a long time at the manila envelope.

Finally, he opened it and began to read.

CHAPTER SEVEN

"Is it . . . is it really you, Daul?"

Araby stared at the clean-shaven man who stood at her apartment door dressed in brown slacks and a tan polo shirt. Same gray twinkling eyes. Same broad shoulders. Same dazzling smile.

But there were obvious differences. No beard. No shaggy hair scraping his collar. No sloppy sweatshirt proclaiming "Songwriters Do It with One Hand on the Piano." He looked so . . . civilized. She swallowed the urge to shout "Where is my old-fashioned, wonderfully natural, unpolished Daul, the Daul I fell in love with?" and smiled weakly instead.

"Hi," he began in a serious voice. "I'm from Talent Scouts Unlimited. I hear you have a way with words, Ms. Gilbert. Are you, by the way, related to the Gilbert of Gilbert and Sullivan fame? No? Well, I'm looking for someone who can write love songs, especially schmaltzy ones. I'm crazy about schmaltzy love songs! Incidentally, so is the public. Would you consider coming to work for me?"

Her grin curved widely, and Araby stepped back for him to enter. "I see you're still crazy, after all these weeks." There was a slight cleft in his chin that she had never noticed before because she'd never seen him clean-shaven. She was still adjusting to the new look, unsure if she liked it.

Daul moved inside the room, his eyes never leaving hers. "Well, what did you expect, leaving me at that deserted farmhouse with no one to talk to but the cat . . . and Aunt Lucy. It gets damned lonely out there by yourself. And the bed is cold at night."

"But that's what you wanted, isn't it? To be alone so you could get in the mood to write an award-winning batch of songs." She closed the door and leaned on it, her eyes still captured by his.

"It's what I thought I wanted. I didn't realize how much you inspired me, Araby, until you weren't there."

"Don't tell me you didn't write all those top-of-the-chart songs after I left."

"Oh, I did that, all right. Couldn't help it when I put your words to my music." They came together, his long arms over her shoulders, his fingers digging into her hair. "Just like us, Araby. Pure magic, sweetheart. Your words and my music belong together, just like us. . . ." His lips descended slowly down to hers, so painstakingly slowly that she held her breath in anticipation.

And when they met and sought the perfect fit, Araby swirled into heaven after a long two weeks without Daul. They performed in perfect harmony, the lifting of two spirits in a love song, a love not yet confessed, not even recognized. But they couldn't let go. Couldn't stop the fiery passion that swelled between them. She wanted him more than she had ever wanted any man, more than she realized while she sat at home waiting anxiously for his call, his return.

She opened her lips for his tongue's swift entry and relished his exploration of every sweet inch of her mouth, allowing her tongue to meet his in tempestuous play.

He shifted to cover her face with hot, fervent kisses, inflaming her cheeks and tender eyelids and the sensitive hollow beneath her earlobe. "Oh God, Araby, you taste so sweet. . . ."

She laughed and drew away for a breath. Otherwise, she might insist that he make love to her on the spot! "Always thinking of your stomach!" Her hand stroked the part of him that framed his stomach.

"It isn't my stomach I'm thinking of right now. It's a stronger appetite I want satisfied." He swung her up in his arms. "Where's the attic in this joint? I'm starved for your love, Araby. And I don't think I can wait much longer."

She pointed down the hall while burying her nose against his neck. He smelled so fresh and wonderful, like the pine trees in the forest near the farm, or the mist from the waterfall, or the grass after a rain. Oh, how she had missed him! "Sorry, no attic. It's only a simple bedroom."

"What?" he chuckled as he strode down the narrow hallway. "No attic with mice and cats and turkey track quilts? A simple bedroom with no atmosphere? A place that isn't too hot or too cold? God, it sounds perfect to me!" They rolled together on her neat bedspread, kissing and laughing and caressing.

She tugged his shirt out of his jeans and slipped her hands around his bare ribs. "I've missed you so, Daul."

"Not half as much as I've missed you. . . ." He unbuttoned her blouse and emblazoned her burgeoning breasts with kisses.

"I've missed your jokes. . . ."

He slid the blouse from her shoulders and unfastened her bra. The twin globes fell out into his hands and he caressed them fondly. "I haven't laughed in so long, my face would crack if I even smiled."

"I never thought I'd say this, but I've missed your twanging guitar in the middle of the night. . . ."

His large hands caressed each creamy breast, then moved to unbutton and unzip her slacks. "I've changed to French horn. No more country music for me."

"I've even missed your cooking. . . ."

He pulled her slacks and panties down past her hips. "I've eaten nothing but rose petals and boiled eggs since you left the farm. And it's been hell!"

"I've especially missed your loving, Daul. . . ."

131

His gray eyes danced over her bare feminine curves, his hands following the rounded shapes. "I've been celibate for so long, I'm not sure I can do this."

She laughed low and sexy. "Not to worry. I think we can handle this," she soothed. "The biggest problem here is getting those slacks off you."

With joyous laughter and loving affection they entered the rites of the timeless act of love, whirling in each other's glory. He hovered over her, his hands pressing hers to the bed, preventing her from touching him. She strained against him when his lips closed over each rosy tip, then softly kissed the valley between her breasts. "Daul, don't be selfish. Let me . . . touch you."

He chuckled with pleasure as her body reacted hungrily. "Not yet. I can't . . . stand it." His tongue paid sweet, erotic homage to her feminity, urging her to the brink of her desire.

She moaned softly and opened to receive the fullness of his love. "Oh, Daul . . . Daul!" She clasped him to her, accepting, clinging, feverishly clutching.

He released her hands and buried himself in her, plunging with a vigorous, pent-up passion. "Araby, oh God, Araby!"

With rapid thrusts they reached the peak of their pleasure, each crying the other's name, each feeling a depth of emotion never before experienced. But neither was willing—or able—to admit it.

After the loving they held each other for a long

time, engulfed in an overwhelming sense of belonging and contentment.

"I'm glad to see it doesn't take a special place for us. We just need to be together, Araby."

"But you have to admit the farm is special. That old iron bed in Aunt Lucy's attic has ambience. And history."

"Our history, sweetheart. Ours, together." His hand gently caressed her bare back. "What about your history, Araby?"

"You mean the men in my life?"

"Hmmmm."

"Well, in college, I had a boyfriend. Occasionally we'd slip away for weekends. But we weren't in love, and when he graduated he moved away and that was that."

"What about Gerry?"

"For a while I . . . I thought that I loved Gerry. But he's only interested in a weekend partner. And I . . . I want something more. A lasting relationship. Finally, I realized that I don't really love him."

"Do you still go to bed with him?"

"No. Not anymore. I . . . we, er, well, we're not seeing each other anymore."

Daul's hand raked through her tousled blond hair. "What do you want, Araby? A little house with a picket fence?"

She sighed, smiling. "True love. Something wonderful. Something spectacular."

"The shining knight on a white horse? Don't you

know there's no such thing? You're living in a dream world."

"Maybe. But I can dream, can't I?"

"Sure." His lips breathed hot kisses on her earlobe. "Dreamers make good writers."

"Is that what you are, Daul? A dreamer?"

"Sometimes. But I know the harsh realities of life. Relationships are fleeting."

"You sound like the voice of experience. Have you had many . . . lovers?" She choked on the thought of Daul making love to other women. But of course he had! How naive of her to think otherwise.

"Enough to know that love is fleeting. You said so yourself. You loved one. Then another."

"No, Daul. I never loved either of them. Not really."

"Well, I know all about loving and leaving. I lived with a woman once. I loved her, or thought I did. But she . . . she found another man." He took a deep, heavy breath. "No amount of love could bring her back."

"I'm sorry, Daul." How could any woman in her right mind leave him? Araby wondered.

"Don't be. I learned all about the 'lost-my-woman blues' from experience. I was in such a blue funk afterward, I wrote three blues songs in a row, and all three hit the charts."

"What about now, Daul? What are you writing now?"

"Who knows? Hits, I hope. Time will tell." He rolled off the bed and began to pull on his slacks,

134

apparently dissatisfied with the turn of the conversation.

Araby watched him with sad eyes. She wanted a confession of love. Instead, she saw a man who couldn't admit to love. Maybe he never would. Maybe he didn't know love when it hit him in the face. Araby slipped into her lacy robe and went into the kitchen.

Daul joined her, watching as she moved about, her voluptuous curves barely hidden by the white, misty robe. He remembered that white apparition floating up the attic stairs, bringing a smile, reading poetry, making love. Fleeting! All fleeting!

Araby set steaming cups of coffee on the table and reached for a box of cookies. "Sorry, I'm not much of a cook. But these are very good. Viennese fingers. Orange and chocolate make a good combination. Like us, Daul."

He smiled. She was still the same. No pretenses. Maybe this one wasn't so fleeting, after all. Then again, how could he know for sure? His experience told him different.

In spite of their strained conversation, a mutual feeling of contentment settled between them. This was the way it was supposed to be.

"Did Aunt Lucy bother you after I left the farm?" Araby mused with a smile.

He crunched a Viennese finger and nodded. "These are pretty good, for boxed cookies. I told you, Aunt Lucy and I get along fine. Everything was quite peaceful. In other words, dull. Except for—" He stopped talking while he polished off the cookie.

"What?"

"Mama-cat. She gave birth to twins. Cutest damn little things you ever saw."

"Please, Daul. No schmaltzy stories about the cat."

He eyed her narrowly. "I left them in charge of the barn. I'm willing to guarantee there won't be another mouse within meowing distance."

"Great," she scoffed. "I've really been worried about the mice in the barn! I'm going to sell it. What difference does it make?"

He grew serious. "I hope you don't have a buyer yet, Araby, because I'd like to rent the farm through the winter."

"You don't have to rent it, Daul," she offered gently. "You know the farm's available anytime you want to go up there. I don't plan on putting it on the market until spring. Aren't you finished with the songs for the movie?"

"Oh yes. I've completed the sound track. But there are others in the wind."

"More songs to write? Why, you shaved your main mood-setter." She reached to caress his chin. "I miss your beard."

"I thought you didn't like it."

"I loved it."

"Well, hell, why didn't you say so? I wouldn't have spent two days shaving the damn thing off so slick!"

"I don't know." She shrugged. "I guess we often

don't say the very things we should." Araby was thinking she should tell him how she felt right now. She should tell him of the depth of her love for him, the contentment and excitement she felt whenever she was with him.

"Aw, growing the beard was a mental game I played with myself." He shrugged. "Nothing more. It belongs to the farm, not the city."

She glanced out the window, observing the traffic on the city street below her apartment. "Maybe you're right. Do you have a new contract? Is that why you want to work at the farm?"

"Nothing concrete right now, but we're negotiating. I . . . I'm anxious for you to hear the sound track, Araby. I think you'll like what I've done with them. They're *our* songs, sweetheart. Gilbert and McNeal."

She looked away quickly, then turned back to smile at him. "I'm sure I'll like them. But they're really yours."

His eyes narrowed as he sensed her reluctance. "Legally you have to sign consent forms that the lyrics are yours. And we'll have them copyrighted together."

"No!" Araby responded without thinking and moved uncomfortably around the room, an apparition in flowing white lace. "No, Daul. I gave the poems to you to use as you saw fit. They're completely yours. I . . . I don't want anything to do with them."

He stood up, perplexed and defensive. "That's crazy, Araby. There's money to be made here. It's stupid for you to turn your back on it. And you deserve credit for them. Don't you understand, sweetheart? I used them all. They're yours—ours!"

"No, Daul. You don't understand." She faced him squarely, seriously. "I don't want—" Her hand flew to her mouth to prevent any further denial.

"Don't want your name on them, do you, Araby?"

"Daul, that's not it, exactly."

"I think that's it, precisely."

"Look, Daul, please don't make an issue of this."

He strode back into the bedroom and began putting his shirt back on. "Don't worry about me, Araby. I'll never reveal your secret."

She rushed to his side. "Daul, don't be angry with me. Try to understand this from my viewpoint. It just . . . wouldn't help my career at the university, that's all. And it doesn't matter."

"Sure, I understand," he said tightly as he stuffed his shirt into his slacks and tightened his belt. "Vandy wouldn't give you publication credits for a country-music song but would lay on the plaudits for a poem printed in *Podunk Literary Magazine*. Actually, Araby, I was serious about you giving up your job and becoming a lyricist."

"Give up my professorship?" she gasped, her blue eyes wide. "Why, Daul, I couldn't do that!"

He stuffed his bare feet into his Weejuns and moved toward the door. "Yes, I can see that now."

"Daul, don't leave like this. When—when will I see you again?"

"I really don't know, Araby."

"Please, Daul. This weekend. There's a play at the university I'd like you to see. It's called *The Belle of Amherst*, about the life and work of Emily Dickinson." Her eyes met his in an earnest entreaty. "Please go with me."

"I . . ." He paused and looked into her eyes, an act that proved his undoing.

"Yes." She nodded.

He copied the motion of her head and sighed. "Okay, Araby. I'll go."

She smiled warmly. "Great. It's opening night and there'll be a reception afterward for the cast and staff. So you might want to wear something . . ."

He stiffened and his voice cut into her. "I'll dress appropriately, Araby. Don't worry, I won't embarrass you. And I'll be sure to wash behind my ears!"

"Daul, I didn't mean—"

"I know, Araby. It's a night for city manners. I'll leave my country-bumpkin ways at home." He slammed the door on the way out, wondering why in hell he bothered with this uppity fancy lady, but the aching deep in his heart reminded him why.

Araby spent the evening in misery, wondering what went wrong between them. She had waited so anxiously for Daul's return. When she wanted to dash back out to the farm last weekend, she held herself back, saying he needed time to work alone. And when he arrived at her apartment today she had felt the ultimate blending of their souls. When they made love every bell in heaven rang for her.

It was perfect. And yet they were so different. . . .

Tears welled in her blue eyes and she was suddenly filled with a sense of foreboding. She recalled the day she left the farm to return to the city. Daul's words echoed in her head. *It'll be different there, Araby. . . .*

As she dressed for the play Saturday night Araby set her mind determinedly that things wouldn't be different between her and Daul. She would do everything in her power to retain what they had had on the farm. It had been fun and natural and their love had come easily. Perhaps that was the trouble. It was too easy. Then when the going got rough, when they moved back into the mainstream of their lives, they couldn't make it.

No! She would not admit to that. She'd never been happier than when she'd been at the farm with Daul. She'd looked inward for the first time in years, had been able to accept the crazy notions that Aunt Lucy's spirit abounded in the farmhouse. And she believed that whatever she felt for Daul—was it actually love?—would last.

She passed over her navy shirtwaist with the wide pinstripes for the slinky black jersey with the halter top and wrap skirt. It was a very classy dress, perfect for the theater. Maybe a little dressy for the university theater, but perfect for her. She whirled before the mirror. Daul would call it sexy. Maybe that's why she wanted to wear it.

She spotted the cherry-wood heart on her

140

dresser and, with a smile, raised the lid. . . . *Keep the lovelight glowing . . . In your eyes so blue . . .*

"Oh, Aunt Lucy, what's happening to me?" she spoke aloud to whomever would listen. "I must be willing to resort to anything, including a sexy dress, to keep Daul. Am I trying to manipulate him? Maybe I should fix him a Southern supper of country ham and grits! Find the way to his heart through his stomach! Oh, this is ridiculous! Either this works, and we make it or . . . or what? Let him go?"

The knock on the door ended her one-sided conversation. She slipped her feet into black pumps, closed the music box, and flew to the door.

Daul smiled tightly, looking oh, so handsome in a dark gray sport jacket, navy pants, and a crisp white shirt. "Sexy dress," he said, his gray eyes admiring her.

She met his approving gaze confidently. That was exactly what she hoped he'd say. "You look very nice, too, Daul."

"Don't you want to check behind my ears?"

"Your ears don't concern me!" she teased with a smile and preceded him out the door. *But your heart does!*

The Belle of Amherst was a one-woman play, the actress portraying the entire, tragic life of Emily Dickinson. Araby was caught up in Emily's explanation of why she wrote and her frustrations at not being published. It was a poignant story of the lady Araby knew so well, of the unpublished work during Emily's lifetime, of her eventual resignation to the situation. In the final scene Emily lifted a sewing basket full of her poems, scribbled on various-size scraps of paper, to the audience.

This is my letter to the world
That never wrote to me—
The simple news that nature told—
With tender majesty.

Her message is committed
To hands I cannot see—
For Love of Her—
sweet countrymen—
Judge tenderly of me.

Tears rose in Araby's eyes as she joined the audience in resounding applause, a tribute to a fine performance, a fine re-creation of the poet's tragic life.

The reception after the play was abuzz with phrases like "Great performance!" and "She had us in the palm of her hand throughout the whole experience!" and "I was moved to tears as well as laughter!"

The mood was warm, but Araby felt uneasy. She introduced Daul to the actress as well as to her professorial colleagues. Daul greeted each new acquaintance with aplomb, proving he could converse with anyone. He was at ease, yet there was nothing false in his demeanor. He was himself, in a handsome sport jacket or a rumpled sweatshirt.

142

Araby watched and wished she could be the same. But who was she? What did she want?

In the midst of the crowd she looked up into the ruddy face of her department head and writing mentor, B. Nettington Goodfield. What would he say about her songwriting antics?

"Oh, Dr. Goodfield! I, uh, want you to meet Daul McNeal. Daul, Dr. Goodfield, the head of the English department." She emphasized his title, subconsciously steering Daul away from his own songwriting career.

Dr. Goodfield plunged right into the conversation. "Daul McNeal . . . the name's familiar. Don't I know you? Are you a teacher in some other department at Vanderbilt?"

"No, sir. I'm a songwriter."

Araby's heart plunged to her feet.

But Nettie perked up instantly. "Songwriter? That's where I've heard of you."

"Probably not, Dr. Goodfield," Daul offered, much to Araby's chagrin. "I'm in the country-music field."

"Ah, yes, of course. Some of my favorite music. American folk music at its best."

Araby stared openmouthed at the exchange between the two men. They were as unlike as two people could be, yet they continued a lively banter.

"In fact, I've written a few songs myself," Nettie announced proudly. "Perhaps you'd like to see them. I'd be glad to meet with you sometime, Daul, exchange ideas, discuss this further."

"Certainly, sir. I'd love to. If you'll give me your card I'll get in touch with you."

Nettie dug into his wallet and handed Daul his card with a happy smile. When he finally left Araby hissed, "I can't believe it!"

Daul shrugged casually. "Happens all the time. When they find out I write songs, suddenly everyone has a song or ten they want to show me."

"Well, you don't have to call Nettie back about this."

"Why, Araby, if he's a friend of yours . . ." A small smile quirked his lips as he dug at her discomfort.

"But he's no friend—"

"Araby, sweetheart, watch your language," he admonished as he placed his hand at the small of her back and steered her to a far corner. He glanced sideways at the crowd.

"Nettie has probably never listened to a note of country music in his life!"

"Maybe he's a closet listener."

"I doubt it! What a snob!" She grew more agitated by the minute. "He's the one who directed me to literary publications."

"Well, we certainly don't want to admit to him what a bizarre route you've taken to reach publication!" Daul gave her a rueful glance and motioned toward the crowd. "But don't worry. I won't mention a word about it to any of your *friends.*"

"Daul!" she muttered in frustration, then

glanced up to see another unwelcome face across the room. "Oh no! There's Gerry at the door."

Daul looked in the general direction. "Ah, good ole Gerry. Your . . . er, *friend?*"

She nodded curtly and turned her back to the door. "Actually, we aren't . . . uh, seeing . . . we don't see each other anymore. I told you that."

"I think I understand. You dumped him when you returned home? Gee, that story sounds familiar."

"Well, I realized that we weren't exactly on the same wavelength. He could never understand me or my writing or—"

"Or another lover? Looks like we'll get a chance to discuss it with the man himself," Daul said in a low tone. "He's spotted you and is on his way over."

"I don't want to talk to him! Can't we escape out the back door?" She lifted frantic blue eyes to Daul. "I don't even know why he came. Gerry doesn't give a damn about plays. He probably wanted to see if they filled the theater tonight and if the play has the potential to make money for the university. It must be about money, because that's his only interest."

"Maybe he knew you'd be here and he wanted to see you," Daul offered and nudged her to turn around and face Gerry.

"Hello, Araby." The handsome man with the conservative short haircut and dark suit took her hand, encased it in both of his, and gave no hint of letting go. "How have you been?"

"Fine," she managed to respond as she struggled to pull her hand free. "I want you to meet Daul McNeal. Daul, this is Gerrald Hughes." As the two men shook hands she added, "Gerry's the university comptroller," hoping to steer the conversation into an innocuous direction and away from her.

"Ah"—Daul smiled amiably—"the man who takes care of the money. Nice to meet you, Gerry."

"Likewise, I'm sure," Gerry mumbled, barely giving Daul a glance. "It's good to see you again, Araby. You're looking fine."

"I'm surprised that you came tonight, Gerry. Plays don't usually hold your interest."

"I'll admit, this one was no exception."

"You didn't like it, Gerry? I thought it was wonderful! Most people we've talked to tonight gave it a favorable review."

"Come on, Araby," he scoffed. "Emily Dickinson was a depressed personality and it shows in her work."

"But now you can understand why, Gerry. She was a victim of the times and her circumstances. A woman oppressed. The play wasn't just about her unhappiness. It was about nature and love and—"

"Don't get feministic on me!"

Araby seethed but worked to control her temper. "Regardless of what you think of Emily Dickinson, you'll have to admit Adele's performance tonight was superb."

He shook his head. "It wasn't terribly inspired or dynamic. Her delivery was too simpering, her appeal too sympathetic. The whole thing was a little too . . ."

"A little too schmaltzy, huh, Gerry?" Daul interrupted brusquely.

"Yes, you could say that." Gerry blinked, assuming a prideful expression.

Daul took a step forward and Gerry dropped back a bit. "For your information, Gerry, I like schmaltz. And so does everyone else, apparently! Except you. Course, you're entitled to your own opinion. I was just giving you mine."

Gerry's expression became strained. "Yes, well, er . . ."

"I guess I'm just an old country boy," Daul continued with a heavy drawl, "but looks to me like your opinion isn't valued very highly around here."

Araby's anger gathered fuel as she watched the exchange between Daul and Gerry. "I thought Adele's performance was so terrific, it was almost as if Emily Dickinson were reincarnated on that stage tonight!"

"Are you hinting at a little supernatural influence, Araby?" Gerry arched his eyebrows and looked down his nose at her.

"Maybe so."

"Good God! That's ridiculous!"

Daul stepped between them, his dark head towering over Gerry's. "Pardon me, folks, but could you two have this spirited conversation some other time? We really must be going. Tonight my medium is going to help me communicate with

Great-uncle Harry and I promised Araby she could talk to him. Just a little test exercise, you understand. You will excuse us, won't you, Gerry?" He ushered Araby across the room and out the door.

"Oh God, Daul! I'm sorry about that!" She fell against his arm laughing. "But it was worth every minute to hear that clever exit line!"

"Actually, I wasn't sure where you stood on the subject until Gerry sparked your ire." He opened the car door and helped her slide into the seat.

"I was a little hot, wasn't I?"

He started the motor. "You have a spicy tongue, Fancy Lady."

"You understand me so well, Daul." She snuggled against him.

"Sometimes that can work against you, Araby."

"What the hell does that mean?" She sat upright and stared at him.

"It means I think we need some time to iron out our differences."

"This is it?"

"For a while."

The whosh of the car tires over the pavement was the only sound as they sped down the highway.

"Damn lousy exit line, Daul," Araby grated as she watched the flashing city lights and fought back the tears.

CHAPTER EIGHT

"Is this your friend, Araby? The songwriter I met at the reception after *The Belle of Amherst* a few weeks ago?" Dr. Goodfield's ruddy face appeared inside her office door and he poked a folded newspaper in front of her.

She read the ad:

> At eight o'clock tonight Daul McNeal will be the guest artist at the Rusty Bucket to sing a collection of his hit songs. In addition, he will preview the sound track he recently completed for a new Clint Eastwood movie. Seating is limited, so come early.

Araby nodded, trying to appear calm. "Yes, that's him all right, Dr. Goodfield." Her heart pounded as she scanned the ad again. "He, ah, he said he'd just finished a sound track for a movie. That must be the one." She felt like an actress, pretending she knew nothing about the songs or the movie.

"You know, Araby, he didn't call me about my

songs. I guess I shouldn't have expected him to. He's probably far too busy to fool with the likes of me."

There was a wistful tone to her boss's voice and suddenly Araby felt a compulsory pang of sympathy for the pompous figure before her. He had a song or ten to share and no one wanted them. Especially Daul. The pain of rejection was apparent on his face. She recognized that wounded look, knew it all too well.

For some strange reason Araby felt obliged to try to make excuses. "Yes, Daul's been very busy with this sound track, Dr. Goodfield. He probably just hasn't had time to call you yet. I'm sure he's doing lots of promo, just like this evening's event." *He hasn't even called me since the night of the play!*

"Of course, Araby. I understand."

B. Nettington Goodfield's hang-dog expression was more than Araby could bear. She knew he was working a number on her, but she couldn't refuse his unspoken appeal. After all, he, too, was a writer.

"Dr. Goodfield, I . . . I'll see what I can do to help you. Next time I see him, I'll remind Daul of his promise to you."

Immediately a smile spread across Dr. Goodfield's face. "Would you mention it tonight, Araby?"

"Tonight?"

"When you go to hear his concert tonight. You

are going, aren't you? Surely you wouldn't miss such an important event as this debut!"

"Concert? I doubt if it's like a, uh, regular concert. . . ." Her head whirled with the prospect. Tonight? See Daul tonight? "Well, I hadn't planned . . . that is . . . er, sure, Dr. Goodfield. I'd be glad to. *If* I go."

"Thank you, Araby! I'd be forever grateful! Thank you!"

She watched the balding professor back out of her office with a silly grin creasing his face. What would he say if he knew her poems were already published in the form of a song? Or several songs! What if he knew that those schmaltzy poems of hers were to be a part of this new sound track Daul was promoting?

Surprisingly enough, he'd probably be jealous as hell! And for that very reason she found it impossible to tell him about her published lyrics. At least that's how she relieved her guilty conscience.

All alone with her thoughts, Araby buried her face in her hands. Why did she tell Dr. Goodfield she'd be seeing Daul tonight? She had no intention of going to the Rusty Bucket to hear Daul's performance. *Until this moment.*

Well, why not? She hadn't heard the songs— *their* songs—and it might be fun to hear them. And to see Daul again. The thought of seeing his face, now clean-shaven, and melting in his sexy, gray gaze sent chills down her spine. She didn't realize until this moment how very much she wanted to see him. The songs gave her a good excuse to catch a glimpse tonight of the man she longed for. . . .

Admittedly, theirs had been a rocky affair from the start. However, once she found herself in Daul's arms, life had been happy and wonderful and oh, so sweet. During those halcyon days at the farm, the days when they made love and laughed and found delight in each other and everything around them, life had been simple and pleasant. Just the two of them together.

But real life wasn't simple, nor was it always pleasant. They had work to do, and individual lifestyles that didn't seem to mesh. Since they had returned to Nashville the difficulties, the *differences,* seemed to multiply and loomed larger than ever imagined when they were lovers in Aunt Lucy's iron bed with the turkey tracks quilt. The solution had been to stay apart. He claimed they needed time. Time for what? To work things out? Or to grow apart?

Oh yes, Araby had missed Daul terribly. She hadn't realized how much until the thoughts of seeing him again set her insides stirring.

With mounting excitement Araby closed her books, stacked her papers neatly on the desk, and left the English department building. The decision was made—she wouldn't consider it any longer. She had to see him again.

Located off the beaten track, the Rusty Bucket was one of numerous obscure old buildings turned into performing studios in Nashville. Araby drove down Sixteenth Avenue, past the famed Music

Row section that housed Nashville's recording industry. Spotting the small Rusty Bucket sign out front with Daul McNeal's name inserted beneath, she pulled into the parking lot. A crowd was already beginning to form.

Inside, the house was dark and already smoky. Most of the interior walls had been knocked down and a stage built in the corner of what was once the back bedroom. Several spotlights hung from either side of the room and chairs were placed in a huge semicircle around the stage.

To slip in and watch unobtrusively was Araby's aim tonight. It would have worked, too, if Daul had been backstage, where a normal performer usually stayed until time to go on. The place had a rowdy atmosphere, with people standing in groups talking and joking. It certainly wasn't the usual hushed, preperformance mood of a regular concert. In fact, laughter echoed off the walls, and Araby wondered if Daul would ever be able to quiet this crowd long enough to perform for them.

A waitress approached to take her order. It wasn't a typical nightclub, since Davidson County law prevented liquor to be sold by the drink. Most of the patrons brought their own liquor bottles, though, and bought setups from the establishment. Araby didn't bring a bottle, so she ordered a 7-Up.

A familiar voice caught her ear, and Araby turned around to stare directly into the face of Daul McNeal. What was he doing out here mingling with the audience? Wasn't he nervous?

Why wasn't he backstage getting ready? Oh dear God, he looked wonderful! His dark hair framed his face, the gray eyes were soft and relaxed, and the scruffy beard was making a comeback! She wondered, but didn't ask, if she had anything to do with that change.

She smiled in welcome and had to resist the urge to reach up and caress the scraggly-chinned face. *Oh, Daul! How I've missed you!*

"You're a little out of your element, aren't you, Fancy Lady?"

She shrugged. "I figured I should hear this sound track before Hollywood turns it into a slick production."

"Well, you came to the right place, because tonight's performance will be anything but slick. In fact, it's about the only time you'll hear me sing, except in the shower. Singing is not my thing. Writing is."

"Then why are you doing this?"

"Strictly for promotion. All the music news folks were invited and I see a few have already arrived."

"Then perhaps I should have considered myself lucky to have heard your twanging in the attic instead of complaining of the noise in the middle of the night. Someday, when you're even more famous than you are now, I'll remind myself of those days."

"I tried to convince you of that, but you wouldn't listen," he grinned. "Perhaps I should consider myself lucky to have had you to myself in

154

the attic. I'll never forget the pleasure of your company." He looked at her solemnly and wondered if he should dare add *the pleasure of your love.*

She knew he was referring to their romantic interludes in the old attic and was quietly grateful for the shadowy light in the room. "You said you wanted to use the farm this winter. Do you still go out there?"

"Most every weekend I make a pilgrimage out of town to the quiet countryside. I sure am going to miss the place when you sell it. I might even consider buying it myself."

"You?" She was startled and suddenly overcome with an anxious feeling. Daul taking over the farm? It was a strange thought. Unnerving for some reason. Somehow it seemed okay for a stranger to have it. But Daul . . .

"Well, sure. Anyway, we couldn't let a stranger buy the old house and destroy the ambience of Aunt Lucy's haunt."

"Oh, Daul," she scoffed. "You don't still believe that nonsense, do you?"

"There aren't any chains rattling in the middle of the night or anything like that, but there are certain other signs that she's still around. I think she's a lot like me, though. Lonely."

Araby folded her arms. *Don't talk to me of lonely!* "I think you've spent too much time out there by yourself with no one to talk to but the cat!"

"It isn't a bad way to spend a weekend. You ought to try it sometime."

"I already have, remember?"

"I remember it well."

A commotion behind Daul erupted into specific requests for him to begin his show. With a wink and a tender touch on her arm, Daul murmured, "Don't leave. I'll see you after the show, Fancy Lady. Hope you like our songs."

Araby swallowed hard as she watched Daul amble to the simple, spotlighted stage. Just talking to him and being close again had enlivened every nerve in her body, and it was a shaky hand that brought the plain 7-Up to her dry lips. Suddenly she wished she had brought along a bottle of Tennessee's own Jack Daniel's whiskey.

In an offhanded, casual manner Daul found a comfortable spot for his stool in the center of the unadorned stage and began to tune his guitar. As if by magic the crowd quieted and settled into their seats. A quick look around revealed not more than fifty or so in the audience, but Araby knew that was the maximum the place would hold so it looked crowded. As Daul began to strum the guitar wisps of smoke wafted over his dark head like stretches of angel hair.

She watched him closely, this sensitive, talented man whom she had known so intimately at the farmhouse. God, he looked dynamic, a casual figure in jeans and a plaid sports shirt with the sleeves rolled up to reveal a smattering of dark hair on his forearms. His hair was jet black and neatly trimmed above his shirt collar, but the beard once again filled in the angular lines around his mouth and chin. It was a nice beard, once it was established, but it had a ways to go yet. A few more weekends at the farm and . . . Her mind roamed to their idyllic weeks in the country as she and others in the audience hummed along with his old familiar hit tunes.

At one point the music turned into an all-out sing-along as the audience joined in old favorite hits and sang with Daul. They cheered and whistled rowdily as he meandered from one chart-topping song to another, all composed by Daul McNeal. Many were familiar even to Araby, although she claimed ignorance in the field of country music. Some of the songs were crossover classics and anybody living in Nashville—or any sizable city—during the past few years would have been exposed to them at some time or other.

The newly composed songs brought a renewed quiet as the crowd listened in awed appreciation to their first public airing. Araby was impressed with the beauty of the music, in spite of the fact that it came from a simple acoustical guitar, not a twenty-piece orchestra. Daul's voice carried the tunes gently and with feeling, bringing her poems to life.

Daul was right about them. Her love poems were about a universal kind of love that could apply to any type of relationship. Of course when Daul sang them the listener knew it was of a man's longing for a woman. Daul's gaze encompassed the entire audience, but he sang to Araby. She could feel it. Or maybe she imagined it and wanted his words of love to be for her.

Tears filled her eyes as she listened to Daul sing her words, their beauty enhanced by his music. Suddenly her poems were given a renewed spirit and inner depth. They reached out to touch the hearts of all who listened. And the reaction of the audience was warm and enthusiastic. They responded emotionally, and Daul acknowledged their eager reception with encore after encore.

Just before he ended the laid-back performance, Daul stood and almost shyly addressed the small gathering. "I want to thank you for being so polite and tolerating my inadequate renditions. I'm not a singer, but I'm glad you like these songs enough to sit through an evening of them. I'm sure it's the wonderful, warm response from an audience like you that keeps performers going. Tonight we're lucky to have the lady who collaborated with me on this sound track, the lyricist, Araby Gilbert. Take a bow, Araby."

She gasped at his suggestion and found herself on her feet staring at a cheering crowd. Her head whirred with the noise of the audience and the blatant defiance of her request that she be kept anonymous! How could he do such a thing? She had asked him, demanded that he take full credit himself, that her name not be associated with those songs. But now, even though this crowd was small, word would travel fast. Daul had a collaborator, a lyricist. And obviously he had no intention of keeping all the glory to himself.

When the show was over Araby pushed her way forward through the gathering crowd of reporters and followed Daul backstage.

"In here," he directed when he saw her.

She ducked inside a doorway and found herself squeezed into the bathroom with Daul. It was the room adjoining the stage and the only one available to serve as a dressing room.

"Why did you do that?" She confronted him, trying to ignore their strange surroundings.

Daul leaned tiredly against the sink and let her ramble on while he wiped perspiration from his brow with a hand towel.

"How could you? I said you could use those poems. They were a gift! Now everybody knows! I want to see that sheet music!" She snatched the music from his grasp and gaped at the front. Beneath each song title was the credit, Gilbert and McNeal! *Gilbert and McNeal!* "Who gave you the right . . ."

He looked at her quietly, without a word.

"Why?" she demanded, tapping the sheets gripped tightly in her hand. "Why did you do this? I told you I didn't want my name on them!"

His answer was slow and reserved. "It just didn't seem right for me to take full credit, Araby."

"But I wanted you to!"

"Legally you deserve a portion of the credit and the royalties."

"Legally?" Her blue eyes darkened with her ire.

"Actually you used them without my signed permission! I could sue you for that!"

He nodded. "Yes, Araby. You can do anything you want about this. I knew it was a risk when I had your name put on them."

"You bet it was a risk. Don't be surprised if you hear from my lawyer tomorrow!"

Daul looked at her coolly. "I figured this deal could go one of two ways. Looks like it flew back in my face."

"Damn you, Daul," she seethed. "You're determined to have things your own way. Well, this time you've gone too far. I can't even trust you!" She whirled around and stormed out into the night wishing she had never shared her poems with him.

"I shouldn't be surprised, Fancy Lady," he mumbled after her. "But I'm damned disappointed that it didn't work."

The next weekend found Daul alone, as usual, at the farm. It was unseasonably cold for Tennessee in November. A chilling breeze whipped across the room, billowing the lacy curtain out like a flag. It flapped above an empty bottle of Jack Daniel's sitting on a wooden box that served as a crude nightstand in the nearly empty attic room.

Daul rolled his dark head restlessly on the pillow, seeking comfort and contentment. He writhed in misery, unable to escape his raging passions. The devil liquor enhanced his wild imaginings of love.

Suddenly a steady hand rested frostily on his brow. He shivered, not so much from the chill as from the searing penetration of her touch.

"Araby, oh sweet Araby! Thank God you're here! I'm dying without you."

"I knew you needed me, Daul. I could feel it. And I need you. That's why I came as soon as I could."

He started to reach for her, but she pushed him back against the bed. "No, I want to make love to you, Daul."

Her lips danced over his face like a million lightning bugs, their gossamer wings flicking from eyelids to cheeks to ears to forehead to chin to lips. He opened his mouth to accept her probing kiss.

"I know what you want, Daul. What you like . . ."

"Yes. Good. That's so nice! Touch me, Araby."

Her hands floated over his body, admiring with light strokes the breadth of his chest . . . the width of his shoulders . . . the tough, flat muscles of his stomach . . . the hardness of his thighs and the soft, sensitive inner flesh. . . . He was burning all over, a flaming volcano building and growing and ready to explode. . . .

"Araby, take it easy, sweetheart!"

"Nice and easy . . ." she repeated and allowed her lips to follow the same path as her exploring fingers did.

The small, moist forays taunted and teased and inflamed him until Daul thought he couldn't stand another fiery touch. Her tongue laved each firm

161

nipple, then roved to dip wantonly into his navel. He gasped for air as she meandered languidly down the dark, central trail to the pounding heart of his masculine energy.

"Araby—"

"I want you, Daul. . . ."

She slipped out of her clothes and slid over him, covering him with the full length of her body, molding her pliable feminine shape to his hard maleness. Her heated skin ignited him with an indistinguishable fire, and he longed for her satisfaction.

"See how perfectly we fit together? How magically we make love? Our love is all that matters, Daul. . . ."

"Yes—yes! Oh God, Araby—"

Fiery pains shot through Daul as the earth, wind, and fire engulfed him, smothering him, and he fought for his life.

Throwing back the quilt and gasping for air, Daul sat bolt upright in the sturdy iron bed with its turkey tracks quilt. "Araby . . . Araby?"

Her name was a mournful sound on his lips as he realized he was all alone.

"Oh dear God, I'm hallucinating. I must be losing my mind. I've been out here with the cats too long. Damn that woman, anyway!" His hand clasped his forehead in a futile effort to ease the pain. Eventually he staggered to the window and let the cool air bathe him.

A stiff breeze caught the lace curtain and whipped it out into the room. The gust knocked the Jack Daniel's bottle off its stand. It was quite cool in the country for November. And lonely.

CHAPTER NINE

"I still haven't heard from your songwriting friend, Araby," Dr. Goodfield said as he perched on her desk.

Araby sighed and looked up into his expectant face. "Dr. Goodfield, I have a confession to make. I did go to Daul's concert the other night. But I forgot to remind him about you and your songs. I'm sorry."

"You went to hear him sing at the Rusty Bucket?" He pursed his lips unhappily. "Perhaps I should have gone with you."

"Perhaps," she gulped, thinking how awful that would have been. How could she explain that when she was with Daul that night, Dr. Goodfield and his songs were the furthest thing from her mind. The last thing she needed was for him to have been present at that concert. He would have discovered that she had written the lyrics of Daul's songs!

"That's all right, Araby," he said genially. "You can do it some other time."

She shook her head tightly. "No, I'm afraid

there won't be another time, Dr. Goodfield. I probably won't be seeing Daul anymore." It hurt to say it, but the truth of the matter was that she had severed whatever relationship they had. It was her own doing, her own *un*-doing, actually.

He did not pick up on her personal revelation. His thoughts centered too much on his own ambitions. "Well, Araby, one thing you learn when you're as old as I am, is that there will be other opportunities. My life won't begin or end because of this country-bumpkin songwriter. Nor will yours, I suppose. Still," he hedged slowly, "it would have been nice for you to do this one little thing for me."

"I'm truly sorry, Dr. Goodfield."

"Someday, Araby, you'll understand the necessity of utilizing every opportunity, whether it's a circumstance or person, to further your goals."

"I'm not sure I understand what you mean." Actually she was beginning to get the picture of B. Nettington Goodfield's ambitions. And she didn't like what was slowly developing one little bit.

"I could write the songs that are on the radio today. They're very simple. Formula stuff!"

"Isn't it possible," she proposed slowly, "that high-quality writing can be found in all forms of literature, including country music?"

"Don't be ridiculous, Araby!"

"But if the songs aren't good the public won't buy them."

"Bah!" he scoffed. "The public can be duped into buying anything."

"I don't agree with you, Dr. Goodfield." She could feel the anger swelling within her. "I think the public knows what it wants. And its taste reflects the times."

"Be reasonable, Araby. Songwriting is a business. And a very lucrative one, I might add."

"So I understand."

"There are big bucks to be made. All I need is the right person to promote me."

"Money? I'm beginning to think that's all you're interested in, Dr. Goodfield."

"Money is a strong motivator, Araby," he admitted with a twinkle in his eye.

Something came over Araby as she talked with her boss. Something revealing and glorious, like the light that accompanies truth. Real truth. And love. Love for a man who was as honest and forthright as anyone she had ever met. A man who believed in the public's taste and choice, who valued its opinion, who longed only to please and entertain. A man who gave her laughter and love and tenderness. Oh, what a fool she'd been.

"What would you say, Dr. Goodfield," she began in a calculating way, "if I told you that I had already collaborated on a few songs with Daul McNeal? That those songs he did for the movie were inspired from my poems—the poems that weren't good enough to be published by the literary presses."

He looked at her aghast. "I don't know if I would believe you, Araby."

"Well, it's true." She shrugged simply. "And I

166

might add modestly that they're damn good songs too. I'll be proud to have my name on them."

"Then I'd say you had probably bastardized your work in order for that to happen."

She stood up and faced him with folded arms and a smug smile. "Why, Dr. Goodfield, you're a hypocrite!"

"Well, what I mean is . . ." He sputtered and began to turn red-faced.

"I know good and well what you mean! It's becoming very clear to me. I've been hypocritical too! I bought that whole ball of wax that you've been spouting about quantity and literary quality! It's okay for you to sell a song because there's money to be made on it. Big bucks, huh? But I should stick to the *Podunk Literary Magazine* that pays in copies!" She pointed a finger accusingly at him. "You know something, Dr. Goodfield? I'd much rather have my work sung by millions than read by a limited number of uptight fools like you."

"For your quality work, Araby—"

"For your information, my quality work is those country-music songs, due to be out on the market soon. I have respect for the public's taste, and for the ability of songwriters." She turned and began shoving things around on the desk.

"Araby, I can tell I've offended you."

"How astute you are, Nettie." She turned around to face him with a sly grin. "Did anyone ever tell you the nickname everyone calls you behind your back? Nettie. That puts you on our level and out of the lofty *doctor* range."

"Why, how insulting . . ." His face deepened a shade at her remarks. "Do you know how long and hard I worked for that title?"

"You know something, *Doctor* Goodfield? I have one of those tags after my name, too, or have you forgotten? You've destroyed my respect for you and the title. When you see Gilbert and McNeal on the album labels and on the movie credits under quality work, remember who *Doctor* Gilbert was! A simple English professor who wrote some damn good poetry! Don't forget the key word—*was!*" A kernel of pride mushroomed inside her and she wished Daul could have heard her. He'd be proud.

"Araby, you're not going to—"

"You'll find my resignation in the mail. Right now, if you'll excuse me, Dr. B. Nettington Goodfield, I have some very important things to do!" She pushed past him and left the building.

Araby drove down West End, her mind churning as she rehashed the events of the last half hour. Actually she was relieved. It was something she needed to get off her chest for a long time. And in the process she saw her relationship with Daul clearly.

She realized her love for him and was positive that she wanted him again. But the problem was in convincing Daul of her love and that they belonged together. She had hurt him. Terribly. She had destroyed the final bridge between them and, worse yet, ridiculed his work. Oh God, what a hypocrite she had been! Would he ever forgive her?

She'd have to work on the convincing. But she had the beginning of an idea that might just work.

Her first stop was to the Jeans Emporium. "I want them tight and worn-looking and . . . very faded," she informed the sales clerk.

The young woman smiled indulgently. "These Levis 701s will shrink to fit when you wash them in hot water. That's the way they're made."

Araby pinched the loose waist and looked into the full-length mirror. "Tight. They must be tighter than this. And their color is far too bright. I want them to look like they've been used."

"If you do exactly as I tell you, they'll shrink to fit your shape perfectly. And with a little work you can make them fade to a pale blue. They'll look like they're ten years old."

"Yes, that's exactly what I want!" Araby nodded enthusiastically.

The young salesgirl's eyes twinkled. "Well, first you wash them in very hot water. Two or three times, at least. Then you take clorox and . . ."

Araby's next stop was in the local sports equipment shop. "I think the navy will make the best background for what I want. I'll take this long-sleeved one. Now where can I get this sweatshirt monogrammed?"

"Monogrammed?" The salesclerk looked at her strangely.

"Yes. I want to have something special printed on it."

"Oh." He smiled with satisfaction. "You need the shirt shop down the street. Next block. They have one of those heat presses and can put anything you want on it."

"Thank you." She nodded, moving excitedly out the door. "A million thanks!"

Araby arrived home with her prized purchases and began her lengthy task. It would take some time, according to the salesgirl. But if it worked, it would be worth every hour. She mixed and measured, poked and prodded, cut and clipped. Finally, hours later, the project was complete. The products were as close to perfection as she could get them. She lifted the shirt against her breasts and looked approvingly into the mirror. She smiled. So far, so good.

Now for the test. She picked up the phone and rang Daul's Nashville apartment. But no one answered.

Daul placed two bowls on the kitchen floor. "Okay, you beasts. Come and get it! Straight out of the can to your lips! Now, I ask you, where are you gonna get service like this when I'm gone? Wonderful rich-smelling fish liver with platypus gravy! I'll tell you! Nobody's gonna give a damn! Certainly not Araby or whoever buys this crazy place!"

He paused expectantly, but the ungrateful cats just continued to eat, never once looking up until the bowls had been licked clean.

Daul poured himself another cup of strong,

black coffee and shuffled over to the kitchen table. "You know about females, Mama-cat. Tell me the truth. I can take it. Just when I thought I had her, she slipped through my fingers. When I thought she'd be so happy, that she couldn't resist our love, she turned me down. When I thought I'd go crazy if I didn't hold her once more, she said, 'Go to hell, Daul!' Well, she didn't actually say that. She's far too classy. But her eyes did. And now, sucker that I am, I can't seem to do a thing about it but retreat to this damned farm . . . and dream about her."

He stopped his audible harangue long enough to pull a steaming tray of biscuits out of the oven.

"I've got all this great food cooked and no one to enjoy it with. Hell, who can eat when I know she's off somewhere in Nashville? She's probably enjoying some play or concert with the likes of gentleman-Gerry, who doesn't believe in ghosts or in having fun. It must be against his strict rules of life. Or maybe she's writing iambic pentameter lines with gibbering-Goodfield, the one with the red nose and briefcase full of songs for my perusal."

He took a bite of dry biscuit and tossed the rest of it in the sink. "Dammit! My stomach is in one huge knot! I've never been so miserable! Too bad. Good biscuits too!"

With a gesturing fist and his head turned upward, he shouted, "Do you hear me, Aunt Lucy? Daul McNeal is refusing food! And Daul McNeal is sick! But it's all in my head! No it isn't, it's in my heart! See? The way to my heart isn't through my stomach. I have been whipped into a thick lather by your snobbish—excuse me, Aunt Lucy, but it's true—snobbish, blue-eyed niece. The one named Araby Gilbert. The one who thinks she's too good for the likes of me!"

He stalked around the house, ending up in Araby's bedroom. "You know, you were right," he commented quietly to an invisible entity. "We're different, Araby and I. A lot different. And I appreciate the way you pointed it out, by sharing those letters and the heartbreak you had because of unsettled differences between you and Jake. You'd think we'd be smart enough to learn a lesson from your experiences.

"Ah, but we, of this new generation, have minds of our own. We'll make our own decisions and mistakes, thank you, and handle them our own way. And be miserably unhappy in our own lives, just like you. It's our right, you know.

"So much for our little country love affair, Aunt Lucy. I'm in such a blue funk this would be a good time to write a terrific 'lost-my-woman blues' song. But I have better things to do. Like pack up and leave."

He clattered toward his attic retreat followed by a sedate, high-stepping Mama-cat and two frisky kittens. Midway up the narrow, steep staircase, he halted. Mama-cat brushed against his pants leg and the kittens played with his shoe laces.

"Hell, I don't know what I'm doing here. Why am I torturing myself like this? Why stay here another minute, remembering. . . . Why should

I sleep in that bed another night, imagining her in there with me? Sleep? Ha! Why bother trying?

"It's ridiculous to stay on here. I'll go somewhere else to write. Somewhere that doesn't remind me of her every time I look around. Hell, I can write anywhere! I don't need this crazy, stupid farm. And I don't need the snobbish Araby Gilbert."

He continued up the stairs, threw a decrepit duffel bag on the turkey tracks quilt, and began to stuff well-worn, faded jeans and old sweatshirts into it. "I know what you're trying to say, Mamacat. I said I could take it, but I lied. The hardest thing in the world is to accept the fact that Araby just doesn't love me."

CHAPTER TEN

Araby stood tentatively on the old front porch. The rough-hewn wooden chairs and the hanging swing were familiar elements of her childhood times spent on the farm. They were also reminders of warm, romantic, September nights with Daul. Now it was an unseasonably cold November. She pulled her jacket tighter as a gust of wind urged her toward the door.

She raised her fist to knock, then lowered it to the handle. Even if it was locked, she had a key. After all, it was *her* house.

Still, she hesitated. No, it wasn't hers. Not really. Daul had taken possession of the place, just as he took possession of everything he touched. Including her heart. In theory the farm was hers. But in reality the space around here was his. His and Aunt Lucy's. Araby was the intruder. An intruder on her own property. What a strange feeling.

She stared at the door gathering her courage. What if he'd actually taken over? Moved in some furniture? Invited friends from Nashville? Oh dear God, she thought miserably. *What if he has invited another woman here?*

Araby raised her fist again and knocked determinedly, thinking how much things had changed since that day three months ago when Daul McNeal stood on this porch and she was lying at the bottom of the stairs. Before she could organize her speech in her head, he opened the door.

"Araby, what . . . what are you doing here?" He looked down at her, his gray eyes bleary, as if he hadn't slept in many nights. His dark hair was disheveled, his clothes hung on angular shoulders and narrow hips. Araby thought possibly he had lost some weight.

"I'm freezing out here on this porch," she grated amiably. "Aren't you going to invite me into my own house?" Even as she said it she didn't believe it. Daul was in charge here.

"Sure, sure. Come on in," he said, backing away from the door.

She entered slowly, finally tearing her eyes from his to gaze around the nearly empty living room of the old farmhouse. Only the upright piano remained. Daul's duffel bag and guitar case stood propped beside the door. She looked at them for a long moment, realizing with a sinking feeling why they were there. She turned sad, blue eyes back to him. "I had forgotten how empty it looked in here with practically everything gone."

"Is that why you came all the way out here? To move out the remaining stuff?"

"Not really—"

175

"You can, you know," he responded curtly, gesturing toward the items by the door. "Won't bother me a bit. In fact, I was just about to leave."

"Oh." She looked lost and forlorn. Was it too late to salvage anything between them? He was so distant now. And angry. She could feel his resentment.

"Maybe you came to deliver the subpoena yourself, and you just can't bring yourself to say it. Well, hand it over, Araby. I can take it. I'm tough."

"The what?"

"The subpoena. Aren't you going to sue, like you threatened that night at the Rusty Bucket? I'll admit you have grounds. I should never have gone ahead with those copyrights without your permission. I'm guilty."

"Of course not, Daul," she laughed nervously. "I couldn't sue you for . . . that. I . . . I appreciate you being so generous as to, uh, put my name on those songs. The money will come in handy."

"Huh? Is this really you, Araby? The one with the sharp tongue? The one who said, 'Don't dare put my name on those damned songs'? The one who doesn't write for money?" In a surprise gesture he reached out and affectionately caressed her cold cheek.

Araby trembled and leaned quite naturally into his touch. "One and the same. I'm a little chilled after the drive. Could we have a cup of coffee or hot chocolate . . . and talk?"

"Sure. Sorry it's so cold in here, but the heater doesn't work. No oil. And I didn't start a fire in the

176

fireplace today because I've been getting ready to leave. Expected to be gone by now."

"Can you wait? Just a little while?" Her blue eyes looked at him pleadingly.

"Sure." He gestured. "Come on into the kitchen, Araby. I'll fix us some coffee and try to warm the place up a bit."

Araby followed him and spotted the kittens playing in the corner. "Oh, Daul," she reacted spontaneously. "What's this? Mama-cat's offspring?"

She knelt beside the two tiny balls of downy fluff that rolled together, playfully fighting over a ragged linen dishtowel. It was one of those towels with the entire year's calendar printed on it. Like most everything else in the house, it was quite old and faded. The year was barely distinguishable. 1950. Araby wondered if Aunt Lucy had saved the towel because that year was significant to her.

"Yep. Those are the babies." Daul glanced over his shoulder as he primed the coffeepot. "They are so different, it's hard to believe they're siblings."

"Like night and day." Araby nodded and watched them with growing interest.

"Like you and me."

Araby shot Daul a questioning glance, then turned silently back to the cats. One of the little kittens was almost entirely jet black, the other a multicolored replica of the calico mother. One was sleek and elegant; the other a playful, patchwork quilt of colors.

"But they have certain traits that link them to-

177

gether," Daul continued dryly. "Their heritage, for instance. Farm cats. They come from the same station in life. Country bumpkins, you might say."

"They're darling," Araby murmured as she picked up the black one and set it in her lap. It mewed and began to knead her thigh with tiny black paws. "Like us, in a way."

"Like us, Araby?" Daul set the coffeepot on the gas-flamed stove.

"Different. But with country roots."

"Oh," he muttered as if the thought had never occurred to him. He leaned against the counter to watch curiously while Araby fondled the kittens. "The kneading means she likes you. I, uh, took the liberty of naming them. They reminded me of us, too, because they're such an unlikely pair. You're holding Gilbert. She's pretty perfect, except for that one white paw. The calico is the chief trouble-maker. Already dug into a bag of flour and scattered it all over the kitchen floor. What a mess that was! White paw prints everywhere! He's McNeal."

"I like him," Araby said warmly, letting the black kitten crawl off her lap. "At least he's honest. I wouldn't be surprised by any of his antics. While this snobby black one, she pretends a lot, but you can tell she enjoys his antics too. And the white paw makes her obviously flawed. No one is perfect, you know."

"Maybe you're right," Daul observed reflectively as the two kittens rolled over and over on the faded dishtowel, black fluffy fur mingled with a blur of gold and white and rust. "I can't help

178

wondering what'll happen to them when I leave. It's too cold for them in the barn."

Araby stood and had to catch herself from pleading *Please, Daul, don't leave! Not now!* Instead, she said, "They should feel right at home in the attic."

"But I told you I'm leaving," he said curtly and turned to adjust the flame under the wildly perking coffeepot.

"You aren't interested in buying the farm?"

"No." The answer was definite.

"Then don't worry about the cats. I'll make sure they're cared for." She shivered inside her jacket.

"Okay. I bequeath the cats to you, Araby." Daul lit the gas oven and opened the door. "Maybe this'll help warm the place a little."

"That's better." She moved closer to the heated stove. And to Daul.

He gestured to the pan of untouched biscuits. "Would you like a bite to eat? Just made those biscuits this morning. And Mr. Gosset brought over some natural honey from his own bee hive."

"No, thank you. I . . . couldn't eat."

"Neither could I."

She pursed her lips with a sly smile. "Daul McNeal refusing food? I can't believe it!"

"Odd, isn't it?" He grinned weakly.

"Daul, why . . . why are you leaving now? I thought you came up on weekends to write."

"I do. *Did*, I mean."

"But it's only Friday."

"I know what day it is, Araby," he retorted. "I

haven't lost that much contact with the real world." He shook his head and poured their coffee. "This place is no good for me anymore. Too many memories, I guess." He turned his back on her and gazed out the kitchen window at the falling mist.

She looked up quickly. *Maybe there was still a chance!* "I had hoped we could get some work done this weekend, Daul."

"You want me to help you haul the last of the furniture away? Why don't you just call the preacher? Or Mr. Gosset."

"I meant that we should work together on some songs. I have a few lyrics I want you to look at. Everyone has a song or ten in the closet, you know. If you're interested . . ."

He wheeled around. It wasn't so much her words as her tone that excited him. Araby had slipped her jacket off, and he could plainly see her entire costume.

Dirty Nikes. Very faded and worn Levis, no pressed creases. Skintight. Sloppy navy sweatshirt with the sleeves cut off at the elbows. Bold lettering across her chest that read "Music City, U.S.A. Where Songwriters Do It with One Hand on the Piano."

Daul felt wildly giddy. "Damned nice shirt you have there." He threw his head back and laughed, a real, honest-to-God sound from deep within his soul.

Araby propped her hands jauntily on her hips. "I figured," she quipped mockingly, "if I couldn't

180

change the leopard's spots, I'd add a few of my own. I mean the clothes one wears help set the mood for writing, don't you think? Also, the hair." She began to unpin her blond tresses, enabling them to fall down around her shoulders. "I've been letting my hair grow. What do you think? Is it casual enough? Or does it need more tangles?"

He pulled her roughly to him. "Oh hush, Fancy Lady. You don't have to go to all this trouble to get my attention, Araby. I love you just the way you are." He wrapped his long arms around her back and kissed her soundly.

She pressed her length to his and hugged him tightly. "I don't want your attention, Daul. I want your affection. Your love. We have to make sure this collaboration is going to work—"

"Araby, sweetheart, are you serious?" He buried his hands in her silken hair. "Of course you are! You wouldn't go to all this trouble if you didn't mean it."

She slid her arms around his back, pressing his ribs to hers. "I've never been more serious in my life. What I mean to say by all this is that I love you, Daul McNeal. And I'll change my spots for you or do anything necessary to keep your love."

"Oh God, how I've longed to hear those words, Araby. But you don't have to change for me. We can work it out together."

"Do you really think so? That we can collaborate on some songs? You see, I've already resigned from the university and I'm a dead duck if you leave town now."

181

"I'd be a fool to leave town without you. Why, I've been trying to collaborate with you since September." His kisses nibbled sensuously around one earlobe.

"Then I'm hired?"

"Hired? I was thinking of a deal that works on a more equal basis."

"You mean like equal pay for comparable work?"

"More equal than that. Something that works like marriage. I wonder if the local preacher would be willing to do the deed."

"I'm sure he would be happy to sanction our living together in this community. You know how country people are. They place a lot of stock in loyalty. Apple pie and the sanctity of marriage and all that stuff." She smiled happily and nestled her head against his chest. "Oh, Daul, I love you. I've never said it, but I do. And I'm sorry for all the trouble I caused you. Caused us."

He pressed her head to his heart. "I love you so much, Araby sweetheart, I couldn't bear to stay around here another minute without you. Everything reminded me of you. I haven't written a word in weeks."

She looked up, her eyes aglow. "Daul, how beautifully romantic."

"I can come up with some very romantic ideas, Fancy Lady," he gibed with a twinkle in his deep gray eyes. "Right now I'm thinking how romantic it would be to carry you upstairs to that turkey track quilt and make mad, passionate love all afternoon."

"But, Daul, how will we ever get any work done?" she laughed as he swung her up in his arms.

"Who said anything about work? We'll live on love and our royalties from the movie. When they run out we might have to pen a few lines." He moved with long, quick strides.

"Of iambic pentameter . . ." She buried the words against his neck as they disappeared upstairs.

Araby contentedly watched the flames lick around the logs in the fireplace. The room was filled with warmth, driving away the chilled November air. And she was filled with a glow created only by the love she shared with Daul. It was a wonderful feeling to know that the world revolved outside and they were tucked away by themselves where only their love mattered.

"Who would believe we'd have a freak snowstorm at this time of year?" Daul approached from the kitchen balancing two glasses of wine and a bowl of popcorn. He knelt on the mattress they had maneuvered in front of the fireplace in the empty living room and handed Araby a glass.

She took the bowl and placed it between them. "After all the other crazy things that have happened to us in this house, I'm not surprised by a little November snow. Seems perfectly normal to me."

Daul scooted down on the mattress and reached for a handful of popcorn. "Perfectly nice and warm. Moving the mattress into the living room was a stroke of genius. Do you know how cold it is in the rest of the house?"

"No," she giggled. "And I don't intend to find out! I have no plans to move from here all day long!"

"What kind of crazy things around here were you talking about, Araby?"

She snuggled against his outstretched arm. "Oh, like the times I thought I heard Aunt Lucy. And the bittersweet irony of her love letters. And us."

"Us? I thought we had that all straightened out."

"We do. You're probably right about my job at Vandy. I should stick it out this year, then reevaluate. My work on Emily Dickinson is too important for me to drop it completely. I can't—shouldn't—abandon her now. We can still work together when we need to on songs. Marriage will help that."

"Did the preacher agree to perform the 'I do's'?"

"Goodness, yes! Tomorrow, after church. He'll be most happy to make our relationship legal and proper!"

"Do you want to invite anyone special to our wedding, Araby? Maybe a few friends from Nashville?"

"Well, perhaps I should ask Nettie to give me away," she laughed. "Especially since this is all his fault!"

184

"How's that?"

"Well, he prodded me into writing, then into trying to get published. That gave me something in common with you, so I'll be forever grateful for those poems. Then, just when I thought things were completely over between us, good ole hypocritical Nettie helped me see myself clearly. And when I was honest with myself I knew that I loved you and our love was all that mattered."

"Then Nettie was able to do what I couldn't!"

"You were too close to the situation, Daul. What about you? I'm sure you have plenty of friends in the music business you'd like to invite over for the ceremony."

"Yes," he pondered. "But I think I'd rather keep this ceremony private and introduce you later as my wife and collaborator at the awards ceremony."

"The what?" she laughed.

"Well, Araby, I just have a special feeling about those songs. We're destined for some kind of music awards. You just wait and see!"

"Oh no! Here we go again with your special *feelings!*"

"Actually, Araby, I have a special feeling about Aunt Lucy right now. Like she's close. In fact, I credit her with showing me that our love was all that mattered."

"Aunt Lucy?" Araby scoffed with a laugh. "What did she do? Speak to you in the middle of the night?"

"No, it was when she spoke to you," he admitted

seriously. "And made sure we read those love letters."

"Oh, Daul, that was all just circumstantial."

"Not so! Those letters were almost shipped out with the furniture," he reminded her.

"Yeeesss, but . . ."

"Surely you don't still doubt her spirit around this house!" He grabbed Araby but directed his comments elsewhere. "Don't look, Aunt Lucy. I'm going to kiss some sense into your doubting niece!"

"Watch it, Daul!" Araby warned laughingly. "You're spilling popcorn all over the bed!"

He hovered over her, gray eyes twinkling. "Hold it! Sounds like a great line for a song—'you can spill popcorn in my bed anytime, baby.'"

"Nope. Too close to the one about crackers."

"Who the hell cares about crackers? They have no taste or sex appeal, anyway. Not like popcorn."

"Sex appeal? Popcorn?"

"No, you!" He covered her face with popcorn-flavored kisses.

"Ohhh, I love it! And you!" She framed his face with her hands and began to kiss him seriously. "I love you so much—" Abruptly she stopped. "What was that noise, Daul?"

"My heart," he murmured softly. "It's a regular snare drum when you kiss me like that."

"No, Daul. Listen . . ." She pushed him away and propped herself up on her elbows. Her blue eyes widened with alarm.

Keep the lovelight glowing . . . in your eyes so blue . . .

186

"It's just Aunt Lucy's music box." His hand slipped around her waist. "Come here to me, my little blue-eyed sweetheart."

"But it couldn't be! I set it up high on the piano," she protested stubbornly.

"Well, the wind just blew it to the floor and the top opened up. That's all."

"The wind? There aren't any windows open! It's too cold!"

"Well, a draft from the fireplace then."

"Daul . . ."

"Maybe it's Aunt Lucy's way of saying she approves." Daul pulled her into his arms and spoke to the invisible entity. "Don't look, Aunt Lucy! This kiss may lead to something else! Like love everlasting!"

Together they sank beneath the hand-quilted covers, oblivious to anything, or anyone, but their complete love.

—You can reserve December's—

Candlelights
before they're published!

💜 You'll have copies set aside for _you_
   the instant they come off press.
💜 You'll save yourself precious shopping
   time by arranging for _home delivery._
💜 You'll feel proud and efficient about
   organizing a system that _guarantees_ delivery.
💜 You'll avoid the disappointment of not
   finding _every_ title you want and need.

ECSTASY SUPREMES $2.75 each

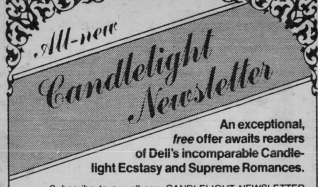

All-new
Candlelight Newsletter

An exceptional, *free* offer awaits readers of Dell's incomparable Candlelight Ecstasy and Supreme Romances.

Subscribe to our all-new CANDLELIGHT NEWSLETTER and you will receive—at absolutely no cost to you—exciting, exclusive information about today's finest romance novels and novelists. You'll be part of a select group to receive sneak previews of upcoming Candlelight Romances, well in advance of publication.

You'll also go behind the scenes to "meet" our Ecstasy and Supreme authors, learning firsthand where they get their ideas and how they made it to the top. News of author appearances and events will be detailed, as well. And contributions from the Candlelight editor will give you the inside scoop on how she makes her decisions about what to publish—and how *you* can try your hand at writing an Ecstasy or Supreme.

You'll find all this and more in Dell's CANDLELIGHT NEWSLETTER. And best of all, *it costs you nothing*. That's right! It's Dell's way of thanking our loyal Candlelight readers and of adding another dimension to your reading enjoyment.

Just fill out the coupon below, return it to us, and look forward to receiving the first of many CANDLELIGHT NEWSLETTERS—overflowing with the kind of excitement that only enhances our romances!

DELL READERS SERVICE—DEPT. B845E
P.O. BOX 1000. PINE BROOK. N.J. 07058

Name_____

Address_____

City_____

State _____ Zip_____